NOON

Editor	DIANE WILLIAMS
Associate Editor	CHRISTINE SCHUTT
Editorial Assistants	REBECCA COLE
	JENNIFER GIESEKING
	REBECCA GODFREY
Designer	SUSAN CARROLL
Business Manager	JUDITH KEENAN
Development Associate	RICK WHITAKER
Copyeditor	MAY JAWDAT
Directors	BILL HAYWARD
	CHRISTINE SCHUTT
	DAVID SLATER
	KATHRYN STALEY
	HAMZA WALKER
	DIANE WILLIAMS

NOON is an independent not-for-profit literary annual published by NOON, Inc.

Subscription price $9.00 (domestic) or $14.00 (foreign)
All donations are tax deductible.

⎯

NOON is distributed by
Ingram Periodicals, Inc., 1240 Heil Quaker Boulevard,
La Vergne, Tennessee 37086 (800) 627-6247 and

Bernhard DeBoer, Inc., 113 East Centre Street,
Nutley, New Jersey 07110 (973) 667-9300

NOON welcomes submissions. Send to:

Diane Williams
NOON   1369 Madison Avenue   PMB 298   New York   New York   10128
Please include the necessary self-addressed, stamped envelope.

ISSN 1526-8055
ISBN 0-9676211-3-5
© 2003 by NOON, Inc.
All rights reserved
Printed in U.S.A.

CONTENTS

THE HEDGES

ॐ

CHRISTINE SCHUTT

The woman who had just been identified as attached to Dick
Hedge looked pained by the clotted, green sound of her little
boy's breathing, an unwell honk that did not blend in with the
sashaying plants and beachy-wet breeze of the island. "Jonathan," she said, and she spoke into the little boy's ear and made
sounds to soothe him, though he would not be soothed. The little boy twisted in her arms to be released. He leaned as far back
and away from her as he could, which the mother said hurt.
"Don't!" she said. "I can't hold you. Jonathan!" She said, "Will
you please hold still?" Luckily for her, she had a husband. Dick
Hedge helped his wife into the waiting golf cart, then took his
place on the other side of Jonathan who, surprised or tired, sat
very still for the ride.

Probably, they did not want to miss the sunset, for they were not long in their cabana. Of course, Lolly Hedge had seen plenty of these sunsets before; she had been to many islands actually. Aruba, Curaçao, St. John, St. Thomas, St. Croix, Little Cayman. Her uncle owned a lot of land in Little Cayman, so the vacation there had been the best trip of them all; like visiting the family compound, everything was free. The best trip, yes. "Except for this one," she said in an obligatory voice or a sad voice or a tired voice—it was hard for anyone listening in to tell. The voice—small, but husky—how to describe it? Lolly's voice was Lolly's most distinguished feature. The woman in front of her smiled, bemused (no doubt by the voice) and told Lolly that the black beans were very piquant and that she, Lolly, should try them. Dick stood just behind his wife holding Jonathan and explaining the food to the boy although the difference between pineapple and mango did not seem to interest Jonathan. Besides, the poor little chap was on this pink medicine, this viscid antibiotic that he often gagged on and which left him sleepy and without an appetite. "Jonathan has been sick for weeks," Lolly said to the woman in front of her. "One of the reasons we decided to come here was to get well."

Lolly was right about the medicine's irritating side effects; Jonathan fussed at dinner and could only be mollified with apple juice, which he drank in a sore slump in the corner of a basket seat. Sometimes Jonathan wagged the bottle by the nipple held between his teeth. He watched his father eat, but whenever he looked at his mother, he whimpered. "Jonathan," she said, sounding exhausted again or sad. "Jonathan, please. Let Mommy be."

The Hedges did not stay for dessert. By then, the sun had set, and the night sky's show was blinking on quickly. A greater darkness amid the foliage squeaked notes, very pretty. In his father's arms again, Jonathan cried and leaned out toward his mother to carry him, but the way was too steep. Lolly did not look at the boy, and she did not speak to him. His father, carrying him, was silent while Jonathan cried against Dick's shoulder and looked back at his trailing mother and never once looked to the nest of cabanas where they were going up and up a hillside of jutting verandas in thin shrubbery.

Lolly must have cribbed the boy in pillows on the bed and slept to one side of him because the next morning Dick was at the front desk arranging for the rental of a crib; there were no other children in sight, and the hotel was not prepared for them.

"At the beach," the concierge said. "Everybody."

Yes, yes, yes, Dick had a wife already there. She was watching from under the palms as her little boy threw sand. Sand gritted his mouth and his bubbly nose. Even the juice in his bottle looked silted. "I give up," Lolly said to her husband, but her husband walked right past her toward Jonathan, making noises of surprise to see him. Dick dropped on his knees in front of the boy and used the long hem of his shirt to clean Jonathan's face, saying, "Hold still," but the boy kept tossing his head until it hurt Jonathan what his father was doing, and he cried.

"Oh, God!" The parents sighed to see Jonathan crab his way to the water.

"Oh, God." This time it was Lolly speaking. "Damnit, Dick—" and she made as if to lift herself out of the web chair as Dick hopped over the already-hot sand toward Jonathan.

"Ouch, ouch, ouch, ouch, ouch," he clowned, and when he caught up to Jonathan he urged the little boy toward the water, but Jonathan did not want to get wet now and held back and was frightened. "I'm going," his father said; nevertheless, when he let go of Jonathan's hand, the little boy cried out, "No!" His voice carried, or so it seemed to his mother as she looked down the beach to where the other early risers lay, and Lolly thought she saw them grimace in her direction. "Dick," she called, "carry him."

Dick reacted slowly and calmly or it might have been that he was simply tired, but he did not rush. He tossed his shirt in the direction of his wife and picked up the crying child and carried him into the water, taking care to keep Jonathan out of the water, putting his own wet hands on the boy's knees and moving his mouth against the boy's face and trying, it seemed, very patiently trying, to get the boy used to it, but Jonathan kept whimpering and holding out his arms for his mother, so Dick said, "All right," and he plunged with the boy into the unfurling wave. He peddled backwards into the foam. "Oh!" Anyone of them said that. "Oh!" Dick was laughing and his wife was scolding from afar, "What are you . . . ." and the little boy was crying and coughing up water.

"It's too cold, Dick!" Lolly stood in the water now with her arms outstretched. "Give him to me." But Dick kept hold of the little boy and bobbed and laughed and seemed smoothly confident he could jolly his son into ease. Lolly, at the shore, kept calling, "Mommy's going to get you," and when she did at last take hold of Jonathan, the small cage of bones that was his chest heaved, so that his mother held him closely and let the boy use her as a bib to rub himself warm against and to clean his face of slaver.

"Someone will be tired," Lolly said as they walked off the beach, but in the end Jonathan's vexations did not make him tired. No mid-morning nap for this boy and not much of a nap after lunch. Usually the medicine made him sleepy, but on their first day at the resort Jonathan stood in the rickety crib the management had found for the family and shook its bars. That was how Lolly described the rout of naptime. She had tried to go on reading on the terrace. She did not look behind her at the swelling curtains; she did not respond to the tuneless xylophone of his bottle banged against the crib slats. Let him rattle, let him cry. Who was there near enough to hear him? They were farther up the mountain in a suite more exclusively pitched. Of course they had paid more. But who wanted to know how much more? They didn't have the most expensive. They didn't have the version with the private lap pool. But the cost of things did not interest Lolly. What she wanted to know was how long did motherhood last? After the noisy beginning of his nap, Jonathan had plumped down onto the mattress. He was making little bubble sounds, and it seemed he was falling asleep, so. So? What was it that made him stand up and cry?

But that was why they were here now, so early, at the pool. The familiar woman from last night's dinner said oh, yes, indeed, she could certainly understand, the boy was . . . well, just look at the boy, so alive, the way he reached for his mother!

Lolly said to the boy, "Daddy will take you."

Sadly, the pool was not as blue as it was in the brochures. On her uncle's island the water was so bright Lolly didn't dare look at it directly.

"Dick," she called out to her husband, "don't you want sunglasses?"

Dick and Jonathan were sitting on the steps into the pool; no one was swimming. Lolly, just behind them on a long chair, was getting sleepy. The whiteness of things—the canvas umbrellas and cabanas, the pool's paved edge—stunned the plants still. The boy and his father were silent. The boy sat in water to his waist and floated his arm on the surface of the water; the father's face was water in a glass, without expression. He said nothing to Lolly's voice, so his wife shut her eyes and woke alone in the shade.

When had they left?

"A long time ago," the nearest guest said.

Itchy, sunburned—Lolly walked unsteadily toward the white glare beyond the palm trees, but when she saw Dick, she turned back for her room before he saw her.

(Later, after the accident, a guest remembered seeing

Lolly walking up the hill from the beach. She was crying. She was crying and unsteady and tripped on a step. The guest said he would have helped but that Lolly was too far away from him, and she was in a hurry and didn't seem to want help. The way her body swiped past staff and guests, he could see her disdain for them.

"The young woman could be supercilious," said the woman who swam with Lolly some mornings.)

Jonathan, on the beach, gouged the sand with a shovel he held like a lance. His father fell asleep. No one saw the little boy walk off, although even Lolly claimed she heard him, and knew he was lost. What crying!

"But I am," Lolly said. "We are," she insisted. She was standing in the buffet line at dinner. Her pert dress had bowtied, string straps and matched the flowers on her sandals. Washed hair, lipstick. Her pale skin was mesmeric and slick under the light of netted globes. Jonathan was not with them. He had been found, bathed, pajamaed; he was asleep. "Lucky us," Lolly said, and then the Hedges ate in silence.

Sometime in the night when the tree frogs had ceased to sing, a cry, followed by another, sounded on the hillside. It might have been a sound of pleasure or pained pleasure or something else; the cry was ambiguous. One of the guests thought it might have been the little boy, the only little boy—the only child—at the resort, but the little boy seemed better the next morning. He could walk; no one carried him into the breakfast room. Jonathan held his mother's hand, and he was subdued, even serene at the table. He sucked on a wedge of toast.

Dick and Lolly looked tired, but after breakfast they took off in a taxi to tour the island. They returned hours later, just after noon. Lolly hoisted herself from the taxi and walked off with her arms held out; she smelled of vomit. She walked quickly to her cabana. No lunch, no tea, no cocktail sunset for her—not even dinner.

"I hope your wife is not unwell," from someone who noticed Dick alone with Jonathan at a dark corner table. Dick said, no, Lolly was asleep, a long day with the baby. Dick said that if they were at home Jonathan would be in bed.

And where was home?

In the middle of the country.

Nothing to be embarrassed about, the man said and looked on as Dick worried the boy's fingers apart to get hold of something speared and plastic. Jonathan fought for it, but once it was lost, he looked around and was distracted, expectant, hopeful as a dog for the next toy, and he got it: a slice of orange from Father's drink to suck on.

Again, in the night, there was a noise, but this time it did sound like a baby.

Lolly was a princess by her own admission; the noisiness of snowscapes, of snow falling or newly fallen, gave her headaches, so that island vacations were best. This was Jonathan's first such vacation, but Lolly confessed she had not considered the meaninglessness of travel for a two-year old. Soft fruit with Cheerios was breakfast anywhere for Jonathan, and he smeared banana into his mouth and gooed his arms and the bib of his shirt. Cereal stuck to him as it would to anything that oozed, and Lolly said she did not want to get near the boy. "Stay away from me," she said in a serious voice, but she smiled at the boy, so it seemed she was joking, and he reached for her again and she screamed. Hardly what had been heard on the hillside last night. Last night's screams had sounded astonished.

Did Lolly like her baby?

Lolly often fell asleep on the job so that whoever was still awake had to care for the little boy, but where was he, Jonathan?

Asleep, asleep.

After that day on the beach when the boy wandered away and discovered he liked the water, for a time at least liked it, on his own, after that day when the boy could have drowned, Dick and Lolly kept Jonathan on the terrace that trembled in the light through the split-leaf fans and flapping foliage. Jonathan played on the terrace with a local girl who saw to it that he was fed.

So Jonathan had a local nanny. How else to explain how blissfully empty-handed Lolly was. "Look at me," and she shut her eyes mid-sentence and fell asleep on the beach.

When she woke, she waved at her husband. "Good luck chasing fish!" she called out to him. Dick was on the ocean for so long—all afternoon—that Lolly went to the dock in search of him, not worried, but curious: and there he was on the boat. There was Dick on the big and tipsy vessel that slowed to the dock. They did not have a camera between them, but the resort took a picture of Dick as he stood next to his fish.

Had Lolly ever heard of a wahoo, for that was what Dick had caught and ordered grilled for dinner.

The dinner could have been photographed, too, but they didn't have a camera. Lolly had seen this scenery before, and Jonathan was sick. She didn't want a picture of a sick little boy. No, when Jonathan was well, then they would buy a camera. For now, for Lolly, it was nice, a treat, a real pleasure to sleep in the sun without worry. It was enough. Shells, shell jewelry, decorated mirrors and flower pots and smoky perfumes, coconut creams and coconut heads and apothecary jars of seaglass and colored sand were so much village junk. She liked to be empty-handed.

Another night Dick sat at dinner alone.

"I hope the family is okay," said the concierge when Dick asked for a doctor he might call in case. But yes, they were okay. His wife was only tired, and the little boy was happiest eating toast with his mother. The little boy was fine, yes. Dick had nothing more to talk about. He wandered into a daze and ate alone and silently, and after dinner he walked the beach. Dick Hedge, a young man with a tired face, sipping a foamy cocktail. He had another cocktail at the bar and still another when the dancing began. He swivelled in his seat to watch everyone partnered. Later when he wove his way through the dancers, the music was louder but some of his words—*don't . . . why . . . can't*—carried and a dancer looked after him: why was the young man so often alone?

After the second day at the resort they penned the little boy in the terrace of their cabana. Lolly said Jonathan just loved Cecilia. Cecilia was courtesy of the resort. Her mother was on staff. Heavy, brown, robustly pretty, Cecilia looked alert enough for a girl, but she was twelve, so was it any wonder? Cecilia and Jonathan were on the terrace every day. She kept the sliding windows open so he could crawl from the terrace to the bedroom and around the bathroom and into the closets. Most of the cabanas on the hill were not large; the Hedges did not have the version with the pool.

The little boy was restless and one day he climbed onto the bed, then onto the tippy dresser chair, then onto the dresser. Cecilia laughed to tell Lolly how she had found Jonathan on the dresser, bumping against the reflection of himself in the dresser mirror, making faces.

Cecilia said, "He sure look he feel something then."

The next day Lolly reported as much to the woman she called the Swimmer. Yes, Jonathan was better. Only one more day on the pink medicine, and wouldn't that be a relief. Then Jonathan might play freely in full sun. Then they could be as a family again. But no more golf! No, Dick would have to squeeze in the holes during naptime, and there would be no more mornings like this one for her. Lolly laughed and the familiar flowered cap nodded back. This woman, the Swimmer, was Lolly's clock. There before anyone else and swimming back and forth and back and forth, this woman held onto the edge of the pool and tried to kick, but her heavy lower body stayed below. She strained to kick and listened to Lolly.

"That's my morning," Lolly said to Dick on the patio at lunch when she was describing the Swimmer. At lunch on the patio Lolly described the Swimmer's struggle in the water, the small splashes that were kicks. Lolly made comparison between her life and the woman's swimming, the struggle to break the surface.

"Jesus," Dick said. He was not in the mood for Lolly's tireless, tiredly lyrical self-analysis. He was flushed; he had played poorly; he wanted a beer. "If that's how you feel," he said.

"My father told me . . . ."

"Your father, your father . . . give me a break."

"I am finding it hard, Dick."

"Hard? What's hard, Lolly?" Dick called over the waiter and ordered his beer. "I know what you could make hard."

Someone at a nearby table overheard this last remark— or maybe all of the remarks—and coughed.

Lolly loudly pushed away from the table and stood up. "I hate this fucking place," she said to the cougher, and then she walked off in the direction of the beach.

(Later, after the accident, this squabble on the patio would be remembered by more than one other guest, and it wasn't the sound of Lolly's voice this time that made the impression. There were others, not just the cougher, who wondered why these two, so lovely and young and clearly comfortable if not rich, why they, with their pouty, pretty son, were so unhappy.

Why did Lolly frown so much?

Why was it Dick drank and drank alone?

Was it their little boy? Was it that they did not know what to do with their little boy? Why had they brought him if they meant to keep him out of sight and in the care of a girl who was clearly unequipped? Why had they selected this resort and not one geared for younger couples and their children?

These were some of the questions some people asked after the accident.)

What was no accident but bad luck was the direction Lolly walked after the incident on the patio because after she left Dick at the table she walked away from the resort, down the strip of beach that came to rock, and then over the rock—she scraped her legs climbing—to the wilder beach growth that scratched. She walked through this brittle, scratchy, wild stuff to the road and continued to walk toward what might become a village. But she never discovered a village because after more than an hour, Dick came up behind her in a taxi. He opened the door and beckoned her inside. "Please," he said. "Something has happened."

Lolly knew enough to get in and that was when he told her.

If she had walked to the cabana instead of toward nothing, the boy might have been saved.

. . .

But who could blame the girl Cecilia? Cecilia was a girl, and Jonathan was a restless, fully mended little boy. One minute he was in the bedroom watching TV with Cecilia, and the next, he was gone to the terrace. Jonathan, the climber, climbed onto the terrace chair and then onto the table and then over the railing. Jonathan fell over twenty feet to the rock path below the terrace. He fell and on the instant died. He fell over the railing and cracked his skull and many other bones that gave him shape.

(Later, the resort guest chorus *ooohed* but stayed away and mostly quiet. "We're on vacation," the guests said. Only Lolly's morning friend, the Swimmer, came forward and saw the couple off. The Swimmer, a woman acquainted with loss, saw the Hedges' sad departure and thought now Lolly Hedge had more than a musical voice; now she had a story, for which in time she might say she was thankful.)

MY HERO, MY MOTHER, MY BOYFRIEND, MY SISTER, MY DOG, MY FRIEND, MY LAND-LORD, MY COLLEAGUE, MY EDITOR, MY FATHER-FIGURE, MY THERAPIST, MYSELF

乄

RICK WHITAKER

---

1. Mid-40s, Caucasian, fake British accent, 5'8", avg. masculinity, straight, clean-shaven, very proper and arrogant, ugly, likes a different girl every night, into light S&M, likes to slap girls in the face, makes her leave barely dressed after fucking, nice apartment, tight with his money.

2. 57, white, a little heavy, avg. height, pretty in a Midwestern way, has had some serious female operations, short black hair, uptight, doesn't like to be touched, likes oral active, likes to be on

top but wants cum all over her face at the end, avg. personality, lots of knickknacks.

3. 30 years old, VGL, uncut, Greek, masculine, vers., not the "gay" type, some hair on chest, smooth legs and butt, large endowment, very horny, ready for anything but no kink, loves to get fucked, likes to cum more than once, likes groups, listens to strange music very loud, lots of wet kissing, sucking, rimming, fucking, no drugs but drinks and smokes, nice sweet guy, likes to talk.

4. Mid-30s, medium height, thin, avg. looks, rough complexion, needs some work on face and hair, wants to be totally dominated, loves hum. and WS, wants to be called a slut, whore, cunt, etc., not into pain, gets upset if hit or pinched too hard, likes to close her eyes and receive oral, but won't spread her legs, married to a gay man, her fourth.

5. Between 2 and 3, was abandoned with broken leg, etc., avg. personality, cute face, very large disgusting vagina and nipples, short hair but it sheds on everything, likes giving oral to males and females, no foreplay, no fucking, lazy.

6. 32, hairy, avg. looks and personality, a little on the fem side, thin, wears glasses, black/brown, about 6', 165, very "sweet" and New Age, hardcore yoga, has a girlfriend but also likes men, into kissing, long and slow, oral active and passive, average cut

endowment, small balls, oozer, likes to rub cum all over his body, likes to get fucked but tight asshole so use your finger for a while, heavy pot smoker, wears girls panties.

7. 60s, fat, very Jewish, heavy accent, ugly, only likes young black trannies who are under the age of 21, oral passive, cut but has a bad smell down there, supposedly rich but nasty apt., says nasty things about his wife.

8. Around 40, short, pretty, JAP, likes rich men even if ugly, only wants vanilla sex, nothing unusual, nice big breasts, scar on her chest, does not like oral passive or active, wants you to cum all the way up inside her and then stay there, watch out for her fingernails, screams when getting fucked.

9. 50s, divorced, rich, pretty, expensive apt., short grayish hair, glasses, fragile pers., likes men with above-avg. endowment, take it slow with her, lots of foreplay and joking around, doesn't like kissing or sucking, likes to talk dirty, wants to get fucked for over an hour in many positions.

10. 60+, avg. looks, Caucasian, a little heavy, smooth, nice boring guy, clean-shaven, divorced with two kids, into heavy-duty coke, wants to be dominated by several men at the same time, tied up to his bed, whipped, likes to have two dicks in his mouth, very loose, can take just about anything up there, fisting, scat, WS, likes to have cum dripping all over him at the end, wife has

"multiple personalities," watches everything while gagged and tied to a chair.

11. Middle-aged, hairy, ugly, European, 5'10", thin, wears the same clothes every day, quiet, not a nice guy, can be very mean and nasty, balding, avg. endowment, oral active, likes to worship body builders, into dirty feet and body odors.

12. Mid-30s, 6'1", avg. looks and person., avg. masc. and endowment, versatile, mostly smooth, short brown hair, low sex drive, likes to watch, into threeways, poppers, porno, massage, seems like he'd rather be doing something else.

BODY

ಎ

OTTESSA MOSHFEGH

I recognize the body was not grown in the country it reminds me of. It lacks the peasant's callus, the roughened hair. Nevertheless it seems fine, moving as it does around the house, in blouses and below-the-knee skirts. We feigned surprise when the joints slid so easily when the body danced, or when the shoulders' bones did not show through the skin under the sun. I recognize the gracelessness of the elbows, the inturnings of the knees. But the body is perfect in this other country. It is best considered here, in this light. Now, in the dark, powered by calves and big-toes, the body takes off itself and shows the body behind the body.

She tells me there are places she doesn't know she comes from.

This is what it feels like to be close to her like that, it is so close like that.

RUBY

༄

OTTESSA MOSHFEGH

Just to watch the hip of her thumb balance the plates as she put away the dishes, or watch the inside segments of her curled fingers collect the crumbs into a pile, every night I died. She didn't know, rubbing salt into the meat, peeling apples, chopping celery, that I was listening. The sounds of her fingers on the wood when she tapped her fingers on the wood said we will keep this between us and then there was music with drums all around. My own hands she guided around, slowly, in the dark, teacher with student, patting me when I paused at the empty curve of her waist—a surprising fall—the weight of her breast, its difference from mine. Even when her hands were empty, I had the feeling that she was carrying something around, a flute of some kind, one that ran on steam, a tiny mouse, a cup of milk. I gave her a ruby ring on her birthday. She received the open box in her palm, the jewel looking very sweet in her hand like that, like a little hard candy. I saw her smile at it for a long while. Then she took some pliers from the drawer and broke the gem from its band. I'll only lose it, was what she said. She lifted her skirt, took the ruby between her fingers, and planted it in the flesh just above her right knee.

She leaned down and blew on the ruby a little.

CORN

჻

OTTESSA MOSHFEGH

Her family was corn people. She was tall as a girl should be when corn grows larger than man. Her father refused to speak the language of food. Corn grew before Christ was born, he said, and threw an ear at the bangboard. Her sisters had small kernel teeth and braided the silk from the husks into ribbon. There was nothing kind in the way she husked corn. She bit with the sure chomp of the cannibal. Only food were the legs and arms of man, she liked to recite. Her hands were never limp on her lap. I never saw her wearing jewels. I cannot describe her manner. I loved the tops of her breasts. She had light brown hair. She did not seem her father's daughter.

Some days she picked, even though her father had the hands. She liked to wear the thumb hook. Of course it was wonderful to watch the girl sweat beside me. When she tired, we sat with our backs against the stalks. Watch me hold my breath, she said. She closed her eyes while she was holding it. I didn't know what to do while she held it. I watched her hold it.

In the evening, she showed me Mercury, low in the sky. That is not a star, she told me. There, they have no water, and no air. A long time ago, she said, kings broke the earth with golden shovels. I knew what she was saying. We went together into the back of the wagon and ate one ear apiece, raw.

KNOT

৵

OTTESSA MOSHFEGH

He sat knotting in the chair made of tin. He liked the fancier knots, the square knots. I cut you loose, he had said. He tied up a half hitch and a single tatted chain. Though his means were poor, his taste was delicate. But here's a young Queen, when she rides abroad, is always knotting threads, he said, and began to cry. He would miss tying granny-knotted ribbons in her hair. He was working roughly with the rope now, burning his hands, letting the loose ends gum up in the mud. He did not think about the children. He tied his last loop. But without her as witness, he thought, who am I to die? He reviewed the world. He unraveled the splice.

STATION

༄

OTTESSA MOSHFEGH

We stand and watch the men pump gas. Their fingers are black and their eyes are greasy. Their heads go up and down while they're leafing off their dollar bills. We like that, we agree. The one we like most is missing a button on his shirt. He is the one with the white arms, like a woman's legs—they get softer as they go up. We can tell he knows we're watching. He puts a little spin on everything. We go one button lower on our shirts too.

I am standing too far away for him to hear me breathing.

I feel older than everybody else.

He has something shiny pinned to his shirt. It sparkles sometimes when he moves. I can't stay here too long without drawing my name in the dirt with my heel. I think he sees me doing it. I rub it out again.

I don't know how sure he is. He couldn't be very old.

He leans up to a window, gives his handprint to the roof of a car with a woman inside. I watch him slouch and wait, his hand going into his pocket, he smiles, she drives away. The girls twist their hair and want to leave now. They start off down the road. He wipes his face off with a rag and opens his mouth. I think I see him watch us go.

SCULPTURE

❧

HENDRIKA SONNENBERG
&
CHRIS HANSON

1 THE IMPORTANT THING IS TO GET THINGS OFF THE GROUND

3 WOOD IN TREES

4 FORT

5 ENTERTAINING PROXIMITY TO MONUMENTS

6 FRUIT BOWL

8 CLOSET ROD

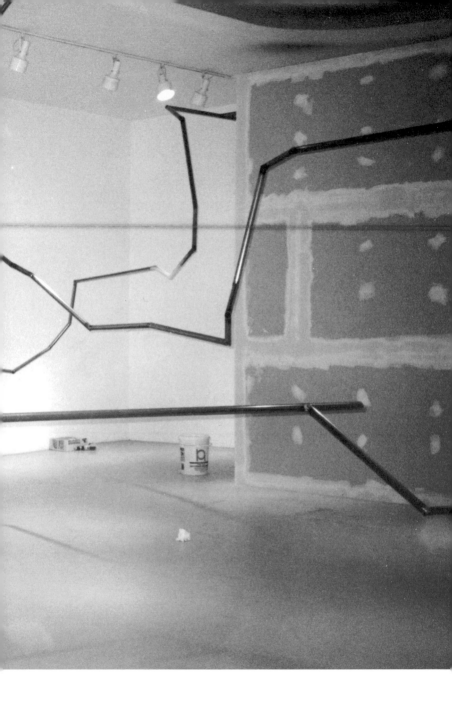

9 LOS STACKOS

10 AGREEMENT ROOM

11 ROUND TABLE

12 DUMPY

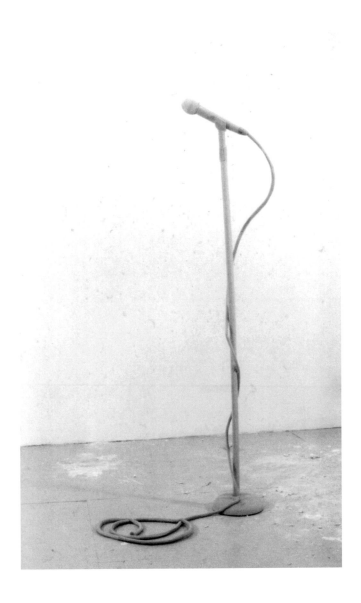

13 SOAP BOX

14 BAUDELAIRE

TODAY IS MY BIRTHDAY

꒛

JIBADE-KHALIL-HUFFMAN

In front of his mother, in front of you; as with the wind knocked out of his dick, he moves you through traffic like the shifting of somewhere now more crowded. Said you'd seen him on the bus one night; said you'd wished something more could've happened—something maybe interesting to tell them about later. You, looking like their mother, hair tied back and sighing; that blank layering of brow and looking at them. Said there'd be more to say if maybe that had happened; said he kept dragging down his jowls with his middle and index fingers—his boy leaning over on his shoulder. Your peacoat a faded red, but still he couldn't bring his eyes toward you—hands in your gray gloves in your small lap—though his eyes still boring into the floor. You wanted him to leave first, to get off a few stops before yours. To watch him walk ahead to the front of the small bus, craning his head down, his son's hand tugging at the side pocket of his coat, out and stumbling upon the sidewalk. On that first night after you got off, watched him up in the window, back turned to you, bus carried away into the going under of the day.

While the others at home look across at you from the porch, the others at home—sister's older son and young daughter, that small house then. With burned up things from the afternoons on the counters and the TV forever handing over the revolvers or there shaking down the bandshells.

Said you'd be along after a while each morning when you left. Mostly asleep then but always the sister and younger daughter when you came in at night. Your sister with those songs, always humming. Those tough cheeks and "When I was a child I had hair down to my butt," to the child. The older boy inside with his shirt off in front of the television, says "Hi" when you come in, then looks away from you. As with his hands in his pants, shifts to the side of the couch, burrowing his arm into its corner, slouching even further. Said he'd like it if you'd tell his mother that seventeen was not too young to have a car, that his dad said he would give him the car, that it would be no trouble; the most anyone says to you all day.

With her hands bounding sideward, skids into his room, and is back on the double with those tapes with the stickers. In confused tenses, looking around and up. Says the boy was hiding tapes with those stickers, and "I can go get them." For no reason, thinks the boy. And leans forward to glare at the child.

Her hands in her lap, his mother looking over at him. In front of her and you, he gets up and into his room he passes. There you hear the "fucks and fucks," and then an "oh, you forgot one of them."

And after this, the boy is off into the late at night. With his own car, with his own keys given to you from the mother just after this scene, you go to pick him up from motel parking lots. You've heard the story of the glasses breaking on the bathroom floor when everyone lost themselves in the glee of pissing, but the boy leaves decidedly before this and on a pay phone risks your help. On the fourth night in a row, after his mother could not hide or hold in her hands or throw from a window the keys to his car, and so handed them to you; again in the parking lot of a motel, as with your fingers slipping from the grip of the steering wheel.

Then the man went on saying nothing, and you got off at later and later stops, until when your sister had seen you walking from the distance, further and further into the evening, after a week you watched him stepping out, saw him not looking up at you, breaking away into the even further off. Then the man again the next night and once more and again until it seems you're coming home only just in time to leave for the motel parking lot.

You see his wife for the first time walking back to the house. You catch them dancing in the large front window, the boy looking on from a chair beside the couch. All this in passing this house several evenings. Said you'd like it better if in some instance he'd see you passing and invite you up to the house. In the office on the breaks, the women stop and stand and pray with you until later you were reported by someone annoyed at the gesture. You watched the man and his wife in the window and then other people passed, out jogging or walking their dogs in the last of light, barely looking up to their right or left or ever even to you.

And since your sister also told you the story of the chance meeting of her and *that* prick and *that* fucker of which only wrong can be said in front of the children, since you say on and on and in trips and passing, it seems things are about to collide; that Car A will smash into the back of Car B and Car B into the back of Car C and so on and Bus A will announce itself reluctantly, in a screeching sort of "Hello" to Cars C and D, and since you know that the mere complicated hierarchy of this happening makes it almost possible, it comes as no surprise then; the swerve and dash of headlight into the yard of the man.

The boy gets out and stands before the window for a moment, before running, and around to the other side of the car, for you, to drag out. Said he told you later that well ahead of this, as he was standing for that moment in front of the window, facing the young boy and his mother, that the man ran out onto the lawn and pulled you out; as with the footfalls as low and stowed as the day he was born, drags you out onto the lawn, clear to the edge of the driveway. Said to you that you were okay, that you were breathing. That people had stopped, Mr. and Mrs. So and So jogging and Mr. Something or Other with his dogs, and they had seen you skidding into the lawn but stopping well before the window.

You hear this repeated over to you again and then again and still yet once more on and through the night and on the buses you hear them for a while going on whispering across from and beside you about your sanctity and the man with his boy and the cups still in the cupboard and beds still in the bedrooms and the living still going on in the living room; holds out his hand to you as he passes to make his way off the bus. In front of the boy tugging at his coat, in front of you; as with the rows left flown and lying over them.

I CAN'T STAND THE SUMMER NIGHTS

࿐

JIBADE-KHALIL-HUFFMAN

The whole town lies down around us. My own worst enemy Johnny dragging along behind me. Says he wants to eat sandwiches so we push each other into the first place we see and sit down. "Oh I'm tired of going on on on about those things, those things," he says and I tell him he's all right while he eyes the guy sitting behind me I think; mumbles into his napkin as I keep going along; spits oranges reds whites, sticky things, into his napkin. When they fall, the hands, some of this drips to his wrists and I just keep looking at him all through his getting up and sitting back down and showing it to me then smearing it into the face of the table and I remember this because I think it's important.

"Just ask everyone," Johnny says. And "Say," I say, and

"Hey," he says back to me and I finally look back over to him. The trouble here was with the love-for-loot girls and Johnny had called the vice squad twenty minutes before, "Just ask everyone," he'd said on the phone, "the bland clad boys just keep knocking and I just keep tellin' 'em." On the television by the bar, Jack Johnson again, fists out in front of his face and next to him Frank, my buddy Frank, going along with the jabs. Falling over, about the girl he says, falling over about his drink he says, "Hey," not bothering to look at either one of us.

I go on about all this to myself, Johnny keeping his eyes on his hands. He leans over after something around an hour. Then tells me and tells me. When I move to get up he gets up. We begin singing along to the tune on the screen. Walking out and somewhere here I think they all stopped and looked up.

And we are gone before the woman can even take down what we wanted. He grabs at my hand at the door and points with my finger to the boys riding by in their cars. Rimming the sides of the streets we see them and start walking in no particular direction, almost toward them. While pausing when one say, had to piss, in an alley stopping, the boys run in circles around their cars and Johnny wonders when they'll ever stop.

On on on back somewhere down the lane we spot Frank arguing with his wife and she's screaming at him for elbowing her in the side. He's tripping over himself and gasping for breath and she just keeps screeching. I tell Frank he's all right in a whisper, so he sits on the curb. Or, or it could've been that Johnny just collapsed into the backseat of one of the boys; with dust sidling into his ears nose mouth it's off putting. But with pinked wrists Johnny knocks me on the back of my legs and I sit down with him and Frank sits down with me and as we stare into the street Frank's wife walks away.

Announced by fluorescence, announced in yawning, announced by his shrug and glare, "Why I think it's—" Johnny tells me. And as he stops I look over to him. Old men scold themselves as they pass us, opening doors, looking in and then turning away thin shouldered so Frank says we should go on ahead. "It's a kind of swiveling of the hips," Johnny says back and of course he had in mind the boys breaking around from out of the corners, right by us. This is enough for him, it's so far but for the once over, giving Frank and me the once over.

It's Johnny and he's saying he's tired of falling from the banisters, that those arms are bruised but that he'd still be good to them if they would look at him again; while they played their way along and away from there. Pawing at me as he says this to make the others look over. They're already in a wide row standing away and outside, running the front of the street, their hands in their pockets; with fists and lips and each other as darlings, darned in graying wardrobes about to fall from the shoulders, saying that there is much to be said for holding on still for this. They're all together and forward before us, with clipped saying for how it happened, how it had stayed on. With an arm and a hand to hold onto my hand, he had them clapping us on our backs with the other hand, asking me then; asking after him, "Say friend, how does that one go again?"

And I say "Hey," and he says, "Say, let's just suppose." Banging his fingers in the middle of a door closing; he comes back over to Frank and shakes his hand, keeping his eye on him for a while.

Standing and then running into an alley and coming out shrugging a blunt board. It's all so far just for the parting, the fop; for all ages and willed for the one and the two and the three.

THE KINGDOM

RICHARD DOKEY

Jerome Conway married late. But it wasn't that he had not always wanted to marry. Every girl he dated at school he imagined in a long, white gown, standing before Reverend Bartholomew, who had confirmed him when he was ten and had presided at his mother's funeral, when she was taken by cancer just before his fourteenth birthday. Since his father Alan, a lawyer with the firm of Langston, Wilfred, and Hume, never remarried and was rather stingy with his affection, the remainder of Jerome's life at home was spent in a formal emptiness, which no friendly cook, cleaning woman, or housekeeper could dispel. The assortment of women that his father sprinkled through his adolescence only left Jerome confused, for no one of them at all like his mother Charisse, whom he remembered so fondly and with such tenderness that every time he thought of her for more than a moment, he wept.

She was tall, but with tiny feet that seemed to float upon the carpet, so that, over the years of tucking him in, placing one last, petaled kiss upon his cheek, then turning out the light, he never once heard her come into or leave his room. Even though he had been unable to bring any of the girls home to meet her, he pretended that he had, imagining little scenes at the dinner table, between the stuffed pheasant and the chocolate mousse, when his mother would ask the right questions. The episodes were clumsy and inconclusive, because, left to his own resources, he could not think what she might say. This was as good a reason as any why he waited. When he was thirty-one and practicing law himself, with the firm of Hardaway and Cuney, his father died of food poisoning in Mexico City.

Jerome inherited everything.

He never really wanted to possess a lot of money. He never really wanted to make a lot of money. The money he had acquired, together with his father's properties and certificates, enough to maintain several families in considerable ease and comfort, only left him feeling oddly bankrupt. He realized, several weeks after his father's funeral, that he was sad, that he had always been sad and that, in some way he could not comprehend, his mother had been taken from him again.

He was, of course, quite eligible, even more so now, and any number of women were introduced to him or found some way to make his acquaintance. He was not manly, though, as his father might say, certainly not handsome, in any accepted sense. But he was not unattractive. In a sweatshirt and jeans he was indistinguishable from anyone else. But he pleased people. Men liked his shyness, his non-assertiveness, which every woman recognized immediately as vulnerability and a kind of incompleteness. If men thought he could be manipulated or cajoled and was not a threat, women intuitively wanted to hold him, then place him near a fire with a warm blanket and a little milk. Jerome felt, then, although he did not understand why, a certain ambivalence, and it was this, as much as anything, that made him leery of close, personal attachment.

But he longed for someone to care for. There was a part of him so deep and unused, so rich and perfect that the release of it would be like a great, new light let loose upon the world. He only needed the right one, the true one for all that love to catch fire.

But he waited eight more years after his father's death before he found her.

The one enjoyment, the one pastime in which he indulged, apart from a certain weakness for imported chocolate, was cigarettes. His father had been an inveterate smoker, Chesterfields, unfiltered, two packs a day. Although he never reached that number, which struck him as flagrant, even dangerous, Jerome permitted himself to consume eighteen, perhaps as many as twenty, cigarettes in the course of a day's work. He spaced them evenly, measuring them by the clock, and looked forward to them, as others do to coffee or tea. In this way he was not addicted to smoking and had convinced himself that something, which in his father's case had been compulsive and, hence, uncontrollable, in his case was always a matter of choice, in other words, desire.

He smoked usually in his office, alone, with the door closed, a carbon device going on his mahogany desk. He kept the cigarettes, a long, slender, filtered blend he had sent from England, in a rectangular cedar box inside the top drawer. He immediately flushed the butt and ashes down his private toilet when he was done and placed a cinnamon-flavored LifeSaver upon his tongue.

There were women. He enjoyed being with women. He enjoyed taking them to dinner or to the theater. He enjoyed sitting near them across a round, wooden table in a dark place, sipping a dry martini and listening to them talk. He enjoyed how they smelled, how they took so much time to be ready, then pretended that it didn't matter, how they always were so interested and self-effacing, how they called him again, even if he saw them only once.

He spent time in bed with a few and enjoyed himself there, but felt always strange afterward, as though someone invisible had tapped him on the shoulder and run away. The effect of this feeling was cumulative, so that he found himself, after a time, experiencing a peculiar separation between body and mind. This made the enjoyment of women more intense, but left him, later, with an alarming sense of failure and betrayal. So, more often than not, he resisted the final plea for intimacy and left them standing at the thresholds of their darkened rooms.

He began to smoke more cigarettes.

He pushed the allotment to twenty-five, then thirty. He kept a full carton of LifeSavers in the desk and was always certain that a fresh roll of them was carried in a breast pocket. When the city council finally voted to outlaw smoking in the workplace, since no ventilation device was adequate to remove all second-hand smoke, Jerome grew desperate. By this time he was almost at two packs a day, and the ghost of his father haunted him at night.

Then he found Elaine Tennyson.

She knew everything she knew from television or those magazines that find their way to the shelves of drugstores. She had wide blue eyes, a complexion natural and unmarred by powder or rouge, and full lips, which she allowed to wear only the faintest hint of red, as if she rubbed them vigorously before each smile.

She was coming by the building that afternoon when he made his three o'clock sprint to the newsstand for a cigarette. He knocked her to the sidewalk.

He picked her up immediately and was so flustered and embarrassed, as much by his own irrational need to smoke as by what he had just done, that he tried frantically to brush her clean. She laughed, showing him perfect white teeth. He forgot his desire for a cigarette and invited her across the street to have a drink at the Italian cafe where he went sometimes for lunch.

He was wearing only a white shirt and striped tie and a

pair of plain loafers. He did not tell her what he did, nor did she ask. She was quite willing, however, to talk about herself. He had never known anyone so straightforward and yet shy. She wouldn't stop smiling, which, he thought, allowed him to see right down into her heart. He asked her to dinner. She consented. He resolved to lie, if only for a short time, about all the money, because there was something genuine in her that he wanted completely to trust. Within four weeks that was accomplished. He proposed to her and she accepted. They were married on a Sunday, only a few days short of two months from that afternoon when he had knocked her down. Reverend Bartholomew, who came out of retirement, performed the ceremony. On his wedding night he told her who he really was and showed her his bank books. She blushed and turned her head into the pillow.

He was overjoyed.

In everything she was simple, tender, honest and loving. Each day when he came home, his rooms were fresh, clean and fragrant. It seemed she always must touch him, caress him, kiss him warmly. In bed she was unbelievably sweet and open, patient and kind. From the moment they began living together, he fell more and more in love.

He even liked her mother, whom he moved to a larger apartment nearby so that visits might be easier. He enjoyed going there for dinner. She was an excellent cook, who created plain, hearty food that he always wanted more of. It was as if his own mother, finally, were smiling at him, as she sent him on his way to rule the life she had so generously provided. He put on weight.

As the weeks passed, he found there was one thing and one thing only that he might change. She would not spend money. She did not like going out without him. It was a large city. There was much to enjoy. He had money. It had no other purpose, now, but her enjoyment.

"Yes, you should go shopping more often," he would say. "You should buy those things that you want."

"But, Sweetheart," she said, "I don't want anything. Really, I don't."

"That isn't the point," he said. "I want to spend money on you. I want you to have nice things. I want you to have everything you ever wanted."

"But, Jerome," she said, "I have you."

"I insist," he said, and deposited fifty thousand dollars for her into a special account.

When he came home one day the following week, she was wearing a diamond about her throat. She lowered her head shyly and blushed.

"Do you like it?" she asked. "Really?"

"It's beautiful," he said. "It doesn't do you justice."

She threw her arms around him and kissed him. "An investment, then," she said. "It's our jewelry. That way we can always turn it in later when we need it."

Throughout that summer and into fall, she, from time to time, showed him a new bauble, which she deposited into a square wooden box.

He was ecstatic.

There was only one thing about him, as well, that she would change: cigarettes. It seemed that she might like a pipe, since pipes could be so warm and aromatic and her father had always used one. But cigarettes smelled so. The odor stayed upon the furniture and the drapes. She smelled it in the bathroom when she went in to shower. Rancid, stale, impure, it was in his mouth at night when they lay down together. And his breath was so lovely, so desirable, she wanted to breathe it coming from the heart of him, wouldn't he please give them up, then, this one thing, for her?

He could not resist.

Immediately he felt healthier. Food tasted better. Colors seemed brighter. The scent of her perfume penetrated untouched places in his brain. Her mouth tasted ripe. He had never thought such happiness was possible.

Then, one afternoon, deep into the storms of winter, she was struck by a drunk driver in a part of the city he hadn't known she visited, and killed instantly.

He would not go into their bedroom. He rented a furnished flat across town. He could not sleep. He spent hours walking about aimlessly. At work he was heard often through the closed door of his office, weeping.

He began to smoke again, one, two, three packs a day. Always he had to have something in his mouth, sucking and pulling. He began to cough. One day, four weeks after his wife's death, the other partners walked into his office and told him he must not come in until he got hold of himself. No one else could work, they said. He calmed himself a bit by lighting yet another cigarette.

"And first," Hardaway said, "you must stop that. You're killing yourself."

The next morning, for the first time in nearly a month, he opened the door to his apartment and stepped inside. He knew exactly what to do, before anything else might go on. He went straight to her dresser and found the simple wooden box. This symbol of everything they intended together must be removed from his life. All the clothing, the knickknacks, the furniture he would have handled by someone else. But the diamonds and pearls, the sapphires and rubies he must take care of himself. The only way to neutralize their power was with a powerful act. To cut himself free of such suffering, he must turn them back into money. Either that, he believed, or forever live with a corpse.

He did not know where she had bought the things, so he took them to the nearest shop he could find. He poured the contents of the box onto the counter and turned his face away.

"How much?" he asked, thinking that, perhaps, he would give everything he got for them to charity.

"These are fake, sir," the jeweler declared. "Imitations. And not very good ones, at that. Not worth more than a thousand at most."

He left everything on the counter and stumbled out the door.

He stared through the window of the shop. The jeweler saw him and raised one arm. He turned and ran.

At the apartment, he looked at each piece of furniture, at every object they had bought. He looked at the backs of pictures and the bottoms of plates. He lifted the chairs and tables. He examined linings, coverings. He took boxes out of the cupboards and read the manufacturers' guarantees. He wanted to know the name on the microwave oven, the refrigerator and stove. He wanted to know who made the throw rugs, the lamps and vases. He picked up the silverware and held it to the light. He rubbed his hands over the cups and saucers. He went into the bedroom.

He turned back the blankets. He felt the pillows. He peered under the bed. He opened the dresser drawers. He pulled out her underthings and nightgowns. He took out the handkerchiefs and scarves. He opened the closets, removed her dresses and suits and placed them one by one upon the bed. He took the boxes of shoes and spilled them onto the floor. In a plastic bag, at the far edge of the topmost shelf, wrapped in a blouse, he found the diary and the passbook, which showed an amount well into six figures. The diary, which he was only barely able to touch, spoke of plans and one he recognized as the manager of a pizza parlor who delivered often to his building.

In the weeks that followed, the world became totally commonplace. Not even the cigarettes he had shipped from England seemed worthy of desire. He gave them up and began smoking the cheapest he could find, generic brands in black and white boxes, unfiltered, that made him cough again and ruined his appetite. He saw no one, talked to no one. The quality of his work fell drastically.

"It's the inhaling," Hardaway said sternly one afternoon, meeting him in the elevator and listening to him cough. "If you're going to smoke so much, don't inhale. Smoke a pipe. There's a shop on West 35th. Good God, man, you're going to kill yourself."

"I couldn't smoke a pipe," he said.

"Well, cigars, then. You don't inhale cigars."

"I've never smoked a cigar in my life."

"Cigars are all the rage now. There's even a magazine about cigars. Do something, man," Hardaway said. "You'll kill yourself."

It was two more weeks before he found himself in front of the small shop on West 35th. The shop had an emerald green door. An emerald green awning covered a window, behind which was a display of clothing that bore the logos of manufacturers he didn't recognize. He stepped inside.

The smell of tobacco was thick and sweet. Glass cases stood in the center of the room. To the right were leather chairs and an imitation fireplace—on a table, an aluminum coffee urn. There were slanted shelves filled with open boxes of brown-leaved cigars. On the left wall were racks of pipes. Behind a counter stood a portly woman with auburn hair, red cheeks, and a full mouth.

"May I help you, sir?" she called.

She looked like a dumpling that had been meticulously colored. Her eyes were green. Her brows were thin, a bit darker than her hair. Her lipstick came to the corners of her mouth, then turned abruptly to the side, just enough to make her smile even broader. She had very white teeth. When she spoke, she made breathy puffs because of the way she rolled her tongue.

"I—I don't know."

Above her head was a row of cigarettes. He recognized the brand he had sent to him from England.

"I smoke."

She grinned. "Yessir."

"I don't like a pipe. I've never tried a cigar."

"You're ready for a change," she said.

He liked that.

"Will you trust me, then? And may I recommend something? An Avo Belicoso. Mild. Sweet. Easy to draw. Lovely taste." She turned and opened a glass door to a small cabinet. "I'll cut it for you. Sit by the fireplace. Have a cup of coffee. Enjoy. By the way," she laughed, "don't inhale. My name is Virginia."

When he lit the cigar, he felt an intense sensation upon his tongue, which immediately retreated to a warm, earthy taste that was pleasurable. The flavor settled into a soft, gentle heat at the back of his mouth. He looked at the woman behind the counter and nodded. She smiled.

He was surprised that she left him alone and was not, at least, curious. At the half hour the door opened, a young boy entered and stepped behind the counter. The woman kissed him, patted him, gave him some money from the till. The boy kissed her in return and left the shop.

He closed his eyes and smoked the cigar.

He came to the shop often, puffing quietly on whatever she recommended.

Her husband had deserted them. He told her that his wife had died in an automobile accident. She invited him to dinner.

He liked very much to be in the shop smoking and drinking coffee. His desire for cigarettes diminished. He stopped coughing. People at work began to smile again.

He enjoyed being in her home, eating dinner there, watching television while, in his room, the boy did his homework. After a time they sat together on the flowered sofa. He smoked cigars and she smiled.

In her presence he felt a calm and certainty he had never known. She had been hurt. He knew she had been hurt, not so much as he, perhaps, but badly, nevertheless, since his own wife was, at least, dead, while that which had harmed her and the boy was still at large. There was something, then, they both understood. Between them a kind of peace and gratitude formed, which, though they never spoke of it, made him believe that she would never betray him. "There ought to be a place," she said, "where every man can smoke a good cigar and not be bothered."

Understanding this, she made his life agreeable. They were married. She never created vulgar scenes with him before his friends. She always told him where she was when she was away without him, so that he never agonized constantly from that time forward.

LIKE IT WAS GOING TO BE

乃

GEOFF BOUVIER

The clearest stories, strung bell-like back from inevitable conclusions, light a present moment to its peaceful end. *When he woke up sober she was gone.* These stories, if they are justified and complete, begin at home—at the end—and return to lead the troubled moment back toward narrative's restful place. *He drank to make her leave him.* The dissonances that might hinder such a dulcet theme—selfish concerns, confusion, laziness, and so on— reduce to a single dissonance, the question of sequence, or rather the question of what sequence will light a particular moment from its own end. *Vanilla, cigarettes, wild almond—her smells— stank into gin.* This end-light shines as darkly as a kind of lack, the lack of alternatives that is called inevitability. *Only an impression in the bed was left to hold him.* For example: I've begun before the suitable end, have not returned here all the way, did not step lightly upon the futures in reversible order, or not all the futures, or not the decisive ones.

ICE CREAM

࿊

KIM CHINQUEE

Hope's father had just beaten her with a stick before going out to do his work. Jen had stood in the hallway while Hope wailed behind the door. Hope didn't know what she'd done wrong, her father just came inside, and started beating her. He did it all the time. After he'd gone back outside to do his work, Hope's mother told the girls they could have some ice cream. She'd said ice cream numbed the pain. So Hope's mom had served the girls two scoops apiece.

Now as Hope and Jen sat outside, licking on their cones, they thought everything would be okay, although Hope was embarrassed and Jen felt sorry for her friend. But they didn't talk about it. Jen was glad her father was nice, and talked to her in his kind voice even when she made mistakes. It seemed like Hope always did things wrong. Now they looked at a frog, and Hope touched him with her toe.

"He's pretty," Jen said. She smiled at her friend.

Then Hope's father walked up to them, and they were afraid. But he wasn't yelling. He held a towel to his face and told Hope to get her mom, so she did, running to the house, and Jen followed. "Go and get your mother," he said again, quietly, standing still, the towel covering his face. Jen and Hope didn't turn back, but when they went outside again, following Hope's mother, they saw blood dripping from the towel.

"Go inside," Hope's mother said. They went into the house, the ice cream dripping down. Some landed on Jen's toe.

Hope's mother drove to the hospital, her husband riding in the passenger seat. The girls sat in the back. They lost their appetites and their cones were getting messy, dripping on their clothes, but they were too scared to ask what to do with them. Hope's father leaned back on the headrest, and held the towel over his bleeding face. Hope's mother sped. Everyone was quiet.

The hospital was ten miles away, in the nearest town. Hope's mother told the girls to wait in the car. They could roll their windows down. "It might be a while," she said to Hope. "Your father cut his face up with a chain saw."

Then Hope's mother and father walked away, her mother holding up her father. Hope had never seen them close before. She'd never seen them touch. She wondered if he'd die.

Hope and Jen threw their cones out of their windows, hoping they wouldn't get in trouble. They wiped their sticky fingers on their shorts.

"He'll be okay," Jen said. She felt sorry for Hope's father, for always being hurt and angry. But she felt more sorry for her friend.

"I know," Hope said. She'd never seen her father hurt before, and she wondered what he'd done in order to be punished. She knew God punished her through her father, at least that's what she'd learned in Sunday school, where she learned the Ten Commandments.

The girls fell asleep. After a couple hours, Hope's parents came back to the car. The girls sat up, sweating, trying to remember where they were. Hope's father had a white patch on his skin, covering the left half of his face, including one green eye. After Hope's mom started the car, her father turned back to look at them. They were scared. They felt sorry for the man. He smiled just like a monster.

71.

EGGS

⅏

KIM CHINQUEE

My mother was a Tupperware lady. She packed her dishes in a big blue suitcase and went off to people's houses, displaying all her goods, handing out door prizes: tokens like pill boxes and popsicle makers for the lucky winners. She talked about these parties. They seemed like so much fun.

At our house, there were dishes everywhere. I had a red Tupperware lunch box that I carried to school, although I'd always wanted a tin one like the other kids, with Barbie posing on the lid, or maybe Raggedy Anne and Andy.

Sometimes Mom would go far for her Tupperware conventions, off to big cities, most of them in other states. She'd stay gone for the whole weekend, up in some hotel. I was in second grade when all this started.

I loved it when Mom would come back with some kind of treat—a new storage box or cereal container—she'd pack it up with a surprise, sometimes little Snickers or peanut M&Ms. She'd take pictures of her weekend, crazy snapshots of her and other ladies, hanging from a barstool, or jumping on the bed, her red hair flying, her arms outstretched just like a plane, and she'd wear her brightest lipstick.

Mom didn't wear makeup when she was at home. There she sat around a lot, eating lots of chocolate, reading the local section of the paper, or maybe *Better Homes and Gardens*. She catered to my father, and told me how to grow up to be a good woman for my future husband. I wondered what it was like for her when she was away.

Before she'd leave, she'd spend a whole day getting ready, soaking in the bathtub, shaving her legs with her pinkish razor. She'd cake a mud mask on her oily face, and manicure her shortened nails. Then she'd go to the beauty shop for a bikini waxing. She packed lots of pretty clothes. She'd leave a cooking schedule on the fridge that was held up by a Piglet magnet— Mom listed the meals I was to prepare for my father, as if he were my husband. He operated his own farm. Mom said we had to keep him fueled, try to make him happy.

On the meal schedule would be the time and date, cooking directions for each detailed item. I did it all myself. I'd try to make each dish perfectly, arrange the table just the way my father wanted, and then I'd eat with him, sitting straight up on my chair, as if at attention. Sometimes my father would rearrange his food with his silver fork, and I'd be afraid I'd be in trouble because his meat was overcooked. He didn't say much about it. He didn't say much of anything, unless he was angry. Sometimes he just looked at me.

One Saturday, I was running late. I was maybe eight. He'd come in from morning chores, and I cracked an egg open on the skillet. I watched the shell break, the egg falling and spreading on the pan. As it fried, I heard the excitement of its sizzle. I flipped the egg, and I could smell my father from behind. He still smelled like the barn. I cracked another egg, sensing his appearance. It splattered on the grill, but it was old and rotten. It reeked and looked an ugly orange and yellow. I didn't know what to do. So I fried it as if there was nothing wrong.

"Throw that thing away," he said.

I took the pan and dumped it in the trashcan. He told me I wasn't good at anything. He smiled at me funny. I felt sorry for the egg. I felt sorry for being such a failure. He told me I better start again. Then he touched me in a secret way. I didn't know what to do. Usually he just scolded me or hit me. This time I closed my eyes, imagining I was somewhere else until everything was over. I don't know how long I pretended. As we ate, I stared at my egg. I wondered how he touched my mother.

When Mom got home, she brought me a plastic Mickey Mouse from Disneyland.

"I had so much fun," she said. She talked about her airplane ride, and about the newest strainer that Tupperware had made. As she showed me photographs taken from the window of her plane, she pointed to a place, saying it was probably our farm. "See, I was watching you," she said.

She made steak from a cow we had to butcher, and I said I wasn't hungry. "Men like girls with something on their bones," she said. My father looked at her. I ate all my steak. I cleared the table. My father napped, and while my mother unpacked all her pretty clothes, I got catsup on my hands. I put the food away, and I scrubbed the pretty dishes.

OATMEAL

ى

KIM CHINQUEE

I'm on a tight budget, saving on grocery items, thinking of how silly it is to buy expensive things. I've been filling up on water, oatmeal, and tomatoes from my garden for the last two weeks. And I'm losing weight.

Beethoven plays softly in the background. The sun shines through the window. My baby coos in his metal high chair. He's ten months old and is eating saltine crackers.

It's just the two of us. During the day, I work in an air-conditioned office, filing papers for an overweight attorney, and Jimmy goes to day care, where pretty ladies care for him when he cries for their attention. He wails loudly every time I leave him, and on the way to work, Madonna blasts from the speakers of my car. I sing along, trying to pretend I'm somewhat happy. Today is Saturday, and we are going to the park to feed the seagulls.

Sometimes I think of all the stupid things I've done. I'd get drunk every weekend, spend my Saturdays in misery until I'd go out again, drowning myself in rum and scotch and the best kind of tequila. I'd wind up in someone's bed. That's how Jimmy came along. I don't know his father, couldn't track him down, didn't know one man from another, having sex with strangers, not remembering their names. It was fun, but self-destructive. Then one day I got pregnant.

Now Jimmy sits there, the saltine crackers all balled up in his hands, his blue eyes looking hungrily at mine. I hold my father's handkerchief that was in his pocket when he died. I squeeze it in my fingers, feel the effects of the Downy softener. The police found him in a ditch; he'd drunk himself to death. That was a dozen years ago, when I was still a teen, and that was when I started drinking. Sometimes I couldn't stop.

My oatmeal has gotten cold, but right now I'm not hungry. I want to have a drink, but I've been dry for eighteen months. I look at Jimmy, and he slaps his hands down on his tray. He babbles and he laughs, raises his arms for me to lift him. I hold him close, but he wiggles his way down, out of my exhausted arms. He quickly crawls away, then stops, turns back to look at me, Daddy, and for the first time ever, he addresses me.

BATH

꒐

KIM CHINQUEE

One day when I was six, I was outside with my sister and then I had to use the bathroom. She raced me inside and won, so I waited by the bathroom door, my hands between my legs, trying to stop my pee from coming. I stared at the white wooden door, and told my sister to hurry. But I couldn't hold it and then I felt pee in my panties, then a rush down my thighs. I started crying.

Jill came out of the bathroom and said, "Sorry," then ran upstairs.

My father was in the living room, where he had been visiting with his friend Alex. "Tanya? What is it?" he yelled, and then he came into the hall and found me, and he held my shoulders, squeezing them, lifted me and set me in the tub, as if I were a mannequin in the back room of a store. He got my Raggedy

Anne bath towel that had been hanging on a rack and then dropped it on my puddle, and he took off all my clothes and told me to lie down in the tub and he ran the water, making it the same temperature he used, which was too hot for me. But I didn't tell him that. I just kept on crying.

My father turned off the water and told me to wash myself with soap, so I did and he went out to Alex. I heard them talking and after a while, the water started getting cold, and my skin was getting wrinkled.

Then my father opened the door, and I saw my Raggedy Anne towel still lying on the floor. He pulled the plug out from the tub and as the water whirled in patterns down the drain, I stood, and he grabbed my hand and helped me step out of the tub. Then he opened the cabinet and found a folded yellow towel and tucked it under his strong arm. He picked me up and cradled me like a baby, carrying me out to the living room, where Alex was, and my father lay my wet body on the sofa as if I were a piece of china on display. My soaked body made wet spots on the flowered cushion.

Alex was sitting on the Lazy-Boy.

"She had an accident," my father said. Then he told me to stand up, so I did, and I turned away from Alex. "You don't have to be so shy," my father said. "Why don't you look at him?"

I wondered where my sister was, wished my mother would come home. I turned toward Alex, looking down, and my father dried me with the towel, running the rough cloth across my back and down my legs, over my bottom, then across my front, my chest, and between my legs. I looked up from the square brown patterns on the floor, up at Alex. He smiled at me, and told my father I was pretty. My father said, "I know."

I always wanted to be pretty. I wanted to tell my father "thank you" for saying something nice. I couldn't wait to tell my sister what he'd said.

I did a pirouette for Alex, and then one for my father, and then he put the towel around me and told me to go up to my room.

PHOTOGRAPHS

꒐

BILL HAYWARD

I invited poets, painters, musicians—artists of every kind—into my studio. I gave them all paper, a brush and a bucket of paint and the same request, to tell some bit of truth.

Merlin Larson
Rock climber/artist

83.

Abby Freeman
Actor

85.

Marcus Samuelsson
Chef, Aquavit

Scott Kilgour
Artist

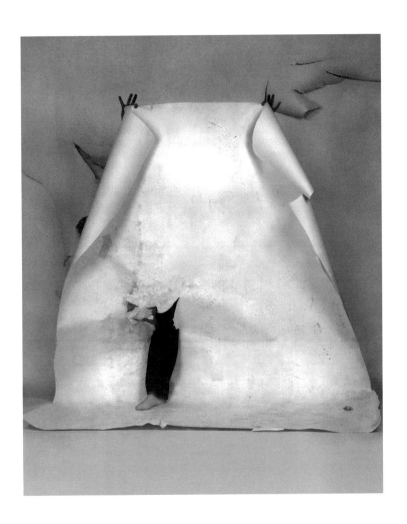

Edgar
"Graphity Artist"

Joanne Baldinger
Painter

Veronica and Oz
Actor and son

Tamara Levinson and Tincho Garcia
Performer/Olympic athlete
Original climber for De La Guarda

Jennifer Allen
Writer

99.

TRANSLATING THE TRANSLATOR

ﾞﾟ

DEB OLIN UNFERTH

Interview with Lydia Davis's Translator,
Ana Rosa González Matute

The occasion for my visit to Ana Rosa González Matute is to talk with her about a selection of Lydia Davis's short shorts that she is translating into Spanish. Davis is a translator herself, usually from the French. She translated one of González's stories from the Span-ish, "Cierta Tarde," *"One Afternoon," which appeared in 2001 in* NOON *along with notes and commentary.*

I meet Ana Rosa at her apartment. Out her window, I look at Mexico City—cement blocks and weathered slabs of pink and white and yellow under a low sky. "Welcome to our contaminated city," she says and hands me a cup of tea.

(This interview has been translated from the Spanish.)

UNFERTH: Can you tell me something about yourself and your background?

GONZÁLEZ: I studied English literature and afterwards, I did a doctorate at *El Colegio de México* in Hispanic literature. I began late. I did other things first.

UNFERTH: What did you do before?

GONZÁLEZ: Dance, modern dance. I lived in London for four years and studied the Martha Graham technique. But I had to give it up because of an accident, a back injury.

UNFERTH: Is that where you learned English?

GONZÁLEZ: Well, first in the United States. I spent my freshman year of high school in Los Angeles. In London I spoke very little English but I always read it. I have relatives who are important writers. One, Salvador Elizondo, who is still alive. He does very complicated work. The other is the poet Enrique González Martínez, who died in 1952. So it was late when I began to write, I was nearly forty.

UNFERTH: You don't look old enough to say that.

GONZÁLEZ: I am the same age as Lydia Davis. We were born in the same year—'47.

UNFERTH: How did you come to know Lydia Davis's work?

GONZÁLEZ: A friend of mine, Roberto Tejada, talked about Lydia. Then I happened to come across her work in a magazine, *New American Writing*, which had several pieces by Lydia that I liked. The first piece I translated was "The Lamplighter." The next was "A Second Chance," an excellent exercise in translation. Oof, it's very difficult to translate. It doesn't seem so when you read it. But the results are very interesting. I did it with my group. I have a group that I do literary translation with. So then I wrote to Lydia and she sent me *Break It Down*. Then I translated "Mr. Burdoff's Visit to Germany" and I included it in my book *Un Caracol en la Estigia* [*A Snail in the Styx*], an anthology of North American writing. It was the first time she was published here in Mexico. Later she sent me *Almost No Memory*.

UNFERTH: What drew you to Lydia Davis?

GONZÁLEZ: She has many stories that are very short, not longer than a page. I saw that in very few words, and with very few turns, she could give a great profundity. One discovers things in her writing. The stories are surprising. And humorous. I like her style very much—how she penetrates the psychology of the characters with an apparent ease.

UNFERTH: Who will be her audience in Mexico and the rest of Latin America?

GONZÁLEZ: I think that here in Mexico good literature is appreciated by a small group. It is not for the masses. I feel that what Lydia does is not something that will be, shall we say, read in the schools, or all over the place, or by the general public, but rather it is for educated readers, cultured people, don't you think? They will appreciate what she's done, will appreciate this capacity of hers to give so much with very few words and in very short pieces. It is something for writers to emulate, for example. Because in general the Hispanic-American story is longer, uses more words, is more baroque, and Lydia's type of writing rarely exists—so concise, so without adornments.

UNFERTH: What problems or challenges have you faced in translating Lydia's work?

GONZÁLEZ: I think that the principle problem—well, I say problem but it isn't really because it has a solution—is that Lydia Davis and other North American prose writers use the repetition of words, such as pronouns, adverbs, and adjectives, as a stylistic technique. Lydia has an abundance of word repetitions. She repeats certain words constantly and in Spanish, in prose, we don't do that. What I had to do was to go to a thesaurus, for example, and look for different possibilities to avoid repeating the same word over and over again. In the case of pronouns, it wasn't such a big problem because in Spanish they are given by the verb. I don't need to say, "*yo corro*" [I run]. I just say, "*corro*," that's fine. Or sometimes pronouns are implied by the adjective. In English, you say, "he is beautiful," or "she is beautiful," but we don't need to say he or she because one says "*bello*," masculine, or "*bella*," feminine. So one doesn't have to put too much emphasis on the pronouns.

UNFERTH: So sometimes you are cutting the repetitions?

GONZÁLEZ: Sometimes, yes. In order that in Spanish it sounds more fluid, more pleasant.

UNFERTH: That's very strange. When I read Lydia Davis, I also notice the repetitions and sometimes I feel uncomfortable with them in English. I think she does it intentionally for various effects—literary, psychological, and philosophical.

GONZÁLEZ: I appreciate the rhythmic pattern and, in this sense, I leave some, but in Spanish it is not the most natural. Maybe I could change a few things. But I insist that in Spanish the result is rare.

UNFERTH: In English it's rare to do it so much too.

GONZÁLEZ: Then it could be a matter of what one thinks. Maybe it would be good to see how it turns out in Spanish with so many repetitions. If it works or doesn't work. I think it would be worth it to see. I wouldn't have to change it very much. Anyway, that's a problem that I had.

UNFERTH: What other problems do you encounter?

GONZÁLEZ: Well, that was the most demanding. Next, the conciseness. When I translate from English to Spanish, the prose lengthens. There are many things that you can say in English in one word, while we have to use three or four. English is more precise. Spanish is more baroque, more redundant. So I try to make the translations as short as I can. For example, in English it is common to have a substantive noun that is not preceded by an article. And in Spanish we have to put in the article. So this lengthens the phrase. Also English has more vocabulary than Spanish. You have words for different things that we don't have so we have to explain them in some other manner.

UNFERTH: Do you have any other difficulties?

GONZÁLEZ: Well, another thing I like very much about Lydia's writing is her sense of humor. So, for example, I remember when I was translating "Mr. Burdoff's Visit to Germany" that I was nearly dying of laughter at certain things. How to preserve this sense of humor? I can't know if I've done it without readers. I can't know if I am communicating this humor, this irony, or if it is lost a little in the translation. I like this characteristic of Lydia's so much. It is such a force. And almost all of her stories have this characteristic, of noticing how ordinary things become amusing. I hope it is not lost.

UNFERTH: I notice that the two languages sound different. Spanish sounds softer. English harder.

GONZÁLEZ: Perhaps. It depends on the sound of a letter, like the "r" in Spanish is more harsh. Or it depends on the combinations of the sounds in the words. Some letters have a stronger sound in English.

UNFERTH: Like the "d" and the "t." Do you think that affects the translation?

GONZÁLEZ: Probably, yes. We would have to see how the piece sounds in English and compare it with the sound of the piece in Spanish. I bet it does, yes. Lydia's words march, one and the other and another and another and again. In Spanish, this is going to be lost a little. But at the same time, it would have another sound that I hope would be as rhythmic as the original.

UNFERTH: Translators always face the problem of abandoning the rhythm to preserve the content. Can you think of an example of a line that required you to make a decision regarding content over sound? How did you resolve it?

GONZÁLEZ: I think that this problem always exists. One has to sacrifice sound and rhythm—the poetry—for the sense. For example in "A Second Chance," Lydia starts out very reiterative. There is a marked rhythm that requires various alterations to translate it into Spanish. The rhythm is going to change in Spanish. And the sound. It is going to be totally different. But this, I will say, is characteristic of all translations. I watch the Spanish carefully because it shouldn't be a struggle to read in Spanish, but should sound natural, and be agreeable for the reader, and understandable. I can't be so worried about the form that it is incomprehensible to read. In this story, "A Second Chance"—but in all of Lydia's stories—you see this. I determine the text this way: I try not to repeat certain words, and if I sacrifice the rhythm I give it a different turn of phrase so that in Spanish it sounds good. So for example, in "A Second Chance," Lydia starts by saying, "If only I had a chance to learn from my mistakes, I would . . . ." Here she is using the first person. But then she changes to the second person. It goes, ". . . . but there are too many things you don't do twice . . . ." and she continues with the second person. This is a problem in Spanish because "you" can be "*tú*," it can be "*usted*," it can be "*ustedes*."

UNFERTH: It could be "*uno*," like "one."

GONZÁLEZ: Well, I thought that this "you" was referring to all people. Like saying, "Look, everybody." So I opted for using the "*nosotros*" in Spanish, or "we." It's more correct. If I had used the "*tú*," I feel that it wouldn't quite fit what she was saying. She wasn't talking about only you in particular. So it seemed correct to me in this case to change the "you." This is an example of how I had to sacrifice—well, more than sacrifice—vary the text.

UNFERTH: I know that you have a background in poetry. In what way do you use your knowledge of poetry to translate Lydia?

GONZÁLEZ: In every way, yes, because it is something I do naturally.

UNFERTH: Do you pay attention to meter and stress count?

GONZÁLEZ: When I write my own pieces, in my poetry, yes. But not in prose. Prose has another kind of rhythm. I pay attention to the phrases, how they sound.

UNFERTH: When you translate, do you believe it is important to know something about the writer?

GONZÁLEZ: On principle, I do not think so, although everything is important. If one can know something about the author, it is better. For example in the case of Paul Bowles, I translated his story "A Distant Episode" and I had already read his autobiography, *Without Stopping*. I am very interested in his life. Knowing about it was a further incentive for me to translate him. But this was an exceptional case because most of the things I have translated—and there are many, by authors throughout North America—I don't know the biographies of the authors. In the case of Lydia, I know almost nothing. I think that it is important to face the author fundamentally through his or her literature. But if one can know something, it's better, right? In this case, I am happy that you talked to me about the repetitions, what she's doing, for example. Because I think that is something that should be taken into account, that she wants the abundance, that it is a question, perhaps, of monotony.

UNFERTH: Do you follow or adhere to a particular critical school? That is to say, do you have an opinion regarding who determines the significance of the text? The author or the reader? Or the translator? Or does the significance change from reader to reader?

GONZÁLEZ: Regarding the critical school, no, not really. I don't adhere to any in particular. But regarding the significance, I think that one fact of being a writer and writing a book is that there is a moment when she must abandon it to the readers. Each reader has the liberty to find whatever significance she wants in the book. All readers are different. That is to say, some have read very little; others, much. Also the reading will be different depending on the age—a younger reader versus an older. Necessarily there is a divorce the moment that the author surrenders her story to the reader. It stops being hers. Something that really caught my attention on this subject is this: My least favorite story in my book *Gneis* is "*Cierta Tarde*" and this is the one Lydia chose to translate. I had said, "I think that I'm going to take out this story because I don't like it" but I left it and now I'm glad I did. When I started to read the translation in English—it had been about two years or more since I had read the story in Spanish—I didn't remember it. Suddenly I read it in English and liked it. I discovered things that I had forgotten.

UNFERTH: What do you think of Lydia's translation? Do you have any comments about her manner of translation or her commentary on the translation?

GONZÁLEZ: Yes, well, for example, the title is "*Cierta Tarde*," and when she translated it, instead of "certain," she said, "one." "One Afternoon." And yes, I liked it because I remembered a song that I don't know if you know, "A Certain Smile" or a movie, "A Certain Smile," ["*Una Cierta Sonrisa*"]. And it was popular years ago. So I felt that it was better, "one," like "*una*," so that they wouldn't seem to come from the same place—the song and the story.

I was also surprised to see that we worked in a similar manner. In a first pass, I, like her, leave the words I don't know in the original language. And later, in the second pass, I go to the dictionary to supply the words I don't know. And later I work on the piece a third time, and a fourth time. Sometimes I have to make many corrections, or sometimes I also, like Lydia, ask people, such as native speakers of English to help me with something I don't understand. So her method of working really caught my attention.

Then in the second version, I saw how the translation was cleaner but still had some loose ends, things that she hadn't yet resolved. At the end of the piece, I say, "*la tierra privada de lluvia, mi tierra privada de lluvia.*" I liked the way she gave it a non-literal translation, "the earth without rain, my earth without rain" [as opposed to a more literal translation, "the earth deprived of rain, my earth deprived of rain"].

She revealed things in the text that I was happy to note. Such as when she notes that "*Caía una ligera llovizna*" [A light drizzle was falling] is redundant because drizzle implies that it is light rain, so why say, "*ligera llovizna*"? But I liked to put it like that in Spanish. It's a question of the sound. And because "*una ligera llovizna*" [a light drizzle] has a connotation that is slightly different from simply "*llovizna*" [a drizzle], or from "*lloviznaba*" [it drizzled].

When I saw the third version with everything complete, I liked her work. I think that the translator has every right to appropriate the text, to recreate it, always, as long as he or she doesn't change the significance of it. It is like a recreation because it is creating at the same time it is translating. So when a translation is really functioning, it is the translator's text in that language. If not, you get a very literal text and that sounds bad in the other language. When I read the third version, I thought with the changes she had made to the phrases, the result was really quite nice. From the first she had respected the sense of the text.

UNFERTH: What do you like about translating?

GONZÁLEZ: Well, I dedicated myself to literary translation I think mostly because I simply enjoy it. But also I feel it is an exercise for the writer. Because when one translates, one has the greatest possibility of penetrating the imagination of another writer, of determining the writer's style and voice. The translator appropriates the text in some way. Inevitably many things are lost in the translation but as a writer, one gains much. So it is part of my formation as a writer because I have been able to assimilate these authors. For example, most writers are confronted with the blank page, right? So in those lapses, when the ideas don't come, and the blank page encircles, it is a way to continue writing. And I have translated many poets and prose writers. Recently I was translating a book by another living North American named Susan Howe. I am finishing the translation of *My Emily Dickinson*. It's a notable study. I suffered much over a poem by Emily Dickinson that begins, "My life has stood a loaded gun."

UNFERTH: Who else have you translated?

GONZÁLEZ: I was translating another poet, another North American, named Ronald Johnson. He has a book called *Ark* that came out not long ago. It's untranslatable into Spanish. I wanted to translate it with my partner, Gabriel Bernal Granados, because he also translates, but we decided that it was impossible to translate the whole book. We translated a selection of poems.

I also translated another complicated poet, H.D. And I translated Paul Bowles and Eudora Welty. And a selection of Walt Whitman. Also some English poets, ancient poetry. Some are the poems put to music by Benjamin Britten in his extraordinary work, *Serenade for Tenor, Horn and Strings, Op.31.* I love English literature and the English language. Now I have very little contact with it. My contact is entirely through the translations. That's why I preferred to do the interview in Spanish.

I was intrigued by González and by her decision, in some cases, not to preserve the parallel structures and repetitions in Davis's work, as one can observe in the piece in these pages, "Una Segunda Oportunidad." *González's argument is that in English, prose writers frequently use repetition as a stylistic technique whereas in Spanish, writers do not. To preserve the repetitions in all cases would make the prose sound unnatural and displeasing to the ear. I admire her boldness and think she has hit on an interesting problem in translation.*

Of course, Spanish prose writers do use repetition. Julio Cortázar's short story, "Queremos Tanto a Glenda" *("We Love Glenda So Much"), is one easy example. The story is structured around a series of variations on the title, such as the following:*

> *1)* "Solamente nosotros queríamos tanto a Glenda" *("Only we loved Glenda so much")*

2) *". . . y quererla tanto a Glenda"* ("... and loving Glenda so much")
3) *". . . éramos tantos los que queríamos a Glenda"* ("... we were so many who loved Glenda")

These variations occur seven or eight times at regular intervals. Within this structure are other systems of repetition at the sentence level, such as, ". . . la última imagen de Glenda en la última escena de la última película" *("the last image of Glenda in the last scene of the last movie") or* ". . . la certidumbre de que el perfeccionamiento de Glenda nos perfeccionaba y perfeccionaba el mundo" *("... the certainty that the perfection of Glenda perfected us and perfected the world"). The repetitions create a hypnotic state while the action in the story moves to a more and more dangerous place.*

Still, as González insists, most Latin prose is more adorned than Davis's—indeed most Anglo-American prose is more adorned than hers, for that matter. In the Cortázar story, many sentences do not repeat so the parallels and repetitions are somewhat masked, while in Davis's stories, sometimes nearly every sentence is a version of the first sentence. The effect of Davis's repetition varies. Sometimes the tone is liturgical, other times fairy-tale-like. Most often the pieces read like recitations of repetitive thought patterns. So the question remains whether one can find examples in the Spanish language where repetition is used in a similar manner.

It occurs to me that the speeches of Latin American politicians, even more so than in the U.S., use similar parallel structures and to similar effects. For example, here is a translated excerpt from a speech by Daniel Ortega that I recorded in Nicaragua during his

2001 presidential election campaign: "We will take back the country!
So that the people may have a new future, so that the people may
have a new hope, so that the people may rise up and triumph with El
Frente Sandinista! " *As with many of Davis's stories, the repetitions*
lead the ear to expect the beginning of a new thought (and therefore
the ending of the last thought), and each phrase feels like a revision
of or an addition to the last thought. I propose, therefore, that
Davis's style of repetition is not unfamiliar to the Latin ear.

One further thought is that possibly this style comes from
Spanish's Romance roots. The local native languages may not ac-
commodate repetitious structures. I recall political rallies in Guate-
mala where the Spanish speaker's slogans rhymed and had rhythm.
But the native-speaker slogans did not rhyme and were very long and
complex and even the chanters had a difficult time remembering them.
I do not know anything about the Mayan-descendent languages and
dialects of Guatemala but it did seem as though the form was unfa-
miliar to these people.

Davis reads the foregoing and adds a few thoughts of her own
and a quesion for Unferth.

I would love to know what those local native languages were. I've
been reading about certain early local French languages and I'm
learning that there used to be, some hundreds of years ago, several
different languages within a fairly limited area (say, the south of
France) and then within each language a multitude of different

dialects with in some cases clear boundaries and in other cases large overlaps. Sometimes just two neighboring villages would share one identifiable dialect, and if you were in Spain, for instance, and met a fellow countryman from your region of France, you would be likely to know which village he came from by the way he talked. So I would guess that this is true, or used to be true, all over, and that Guatemala would have, or used to have, many local dialects that differed slightly or a great deal from one another. I can't believe, though—but I don't know, and it may be quite possible—that the native languages you're talking about didn't use repetition and possibly rhyme fully as much as Spanish (and English), especially in chants or, for instance, proverbs—things one wants to remember.

I'm especially convinced of this because I've just been making my way through a monograph on Malagasy proverbs (I would not have recognized the word "Malagasy" four days ago—it is the adjective qualifying the people of Madagascar) by an ethnographer, one Lee Haring. (The monograph was harder to understand when I tried to read it on a Peter Pan bus while the bus company showed a film—compulsory, in effect, because the sound did not come through earphones but filled the bus—about the real existence of angels, narrated by people who believed in angels, particularly guardian angels, and who told us how to get in touch with our own guardian angels.*) Now Madagascar is around on the other side of the world; and

---

* *The advice was that since our guardian angels are always near us, but inaccessible because of our own resistance to them, we should dedicate a particular spot in the house, like a rocking chair, to be our quiet place where we may be more open to our angels.*

this monograph analyzes, among other things, the use of repetition and parallelism in pithy Malagasy sayings and proverbs:

> ny voanjo boto tsa tamean-tsira
> *the nut whole, salt enters not*
> ny zaza ho gege tsa tamean'anatra
> *the child stubborn, advice enters not.*

But, says Haring, some statements using repetition may not be proverbs, but longer oratorical flourishes:

> *the mountain is the resting-place of the fog*
> *the valley is the resting-place of the mosquito*
> *the creek is the resting-place of the crocodile*
> *and the chief is the resting-place of responsibility.*

Haring differentiates a proverb from a commonsense statement of fact ("There are times when the rain falls right after this sacrifice, and other times when it doesn't come at all," says an experienced old diviner). He points out that as soon as a person uses a certain repetitive form, his hearer prepares to identify what he is saying as a proverb. (He also points out that it may be easier for a son to rely on a proverb to answer his father than a direct personal remark, as in the following. Father: 'You must decide to take a wife; you are of an age to get married.' Son: 'Oh, Father, I don't want people to say, "In a hurry to marry, then in haste to divorce."')

Maybe in the case of your example, the fault was not in the language but in the native speaker himself or herself, who may not have had a gift for composing catchy slogans. It would be fascinating to know more. Look what a door we open when we begin talking about repetition!

Unferth responds.

I suspect you're right. Mayan-descendent languages most likely do use repetition. I don't think, however, that a single person was abnormally bad at creating jingles. I've heard these long rallying cries several times and by different groups and I've heard Spanish speakers and international observers make little jokes about it. I suspect that for some reason the form of political-slogan chant in particular doesn't translate well.

    By the way, there is a Spanish proverb that parallels your final example: "Antes que te cases, mira lo que haces!" *or "Before you marry, watch what you do!" Wisdom across cultures.*

    Of course, these notes are brief and incomplete. Much more could be said. I am grateful to González for opening this discussion and pointing out another difficult area in translation.

UNA SEGUNDA OPORTUNIDAD

༄

LYDIA DAVIS
Translation by Ana Rosa González Matute

Si tuviera la oportunidad de aprender de mis errores lo haría, pero son demasiadas las cosas que no se presentan dos veces; de hecho, las más importantes son irrepetibles, así que es imposible mejorarlas la segunda vez. Cometemos un error, vemos lo que hubiera sido correcto y estaríamos dispuestos a rectificar si se presentara la ocasión; pero la siguiente experiencia es muy distinta, nos equivocamos de nuevo y aunque estuviésemos preparados para afrontar esa situación al momento de repetirse, no lo estamos para la siguiente experiencia. Por ejemplo, si fuera posible casarse a los dieciocho años dos veces, entonces la segunda vez podríamos asegurarnos de no estar demasiado jóvenes para dar el paso, ya que tendríamos la perspectiva de la edad y en tal caso sabríamos que nos aconsejó mal la persona que nos

A SECOND CHANCE

ᡒ

LYDIA DAVIS

If only I had a chance to learn from my mistakes, I would, but there are too many things you don't do twice; in fact, the most important things are the things you don't do twice, so you can't do them better the second time. You do something wrong, and see what the right thing would have been, and are ready to do it, should you have the chance again, but the next experience is quite different, and your judgment is wrong again, and though you are now prepared for this experience should it repeat itself, you are not prepared for the next experience. If only, for instance, you could get married at eighteen twice, then the second time you could make sure you were not too young to do this, because you would have the perspective of being older, and would know that the person advising you to marry this man was giving

animó a casarnos con ese hombre, porque sus razones serían las mismas que nos dio la última vez que nos recomendó casarnos a los dieciocho. Si pudiéramos traer a un hijo del primer matrimonio al segundo matrimonio la segunda vez, sabríamos que la generosidad puede convertirse en resentimiento si no hacemos las cosas correctamente, y el resentimiento podría convertirse en generosidad si lo hiciéramos así, a menos que el hombre con quien nos casamos cuando lo hicimos la segunda vez por segunda vez fuera muy distinto en temperamento al hombre con quien nos casamos la segunda vez por primera vez, en cuyo caso tendríamos que casarnos con él dos veces para aprender lo que hubiera sido más sensato para un hombre con su temperamento. Si fuera posible que nuestra madre muriera una segunda vez estaríamos dispuestos a exigir un cuarto privado sin la presencia de otro enfermo viendo la televisión mientras ella moría; mas en caso de que estuviésemos dispuestos a insistir, tendríamos que perder a nuestra madre una vez más para saber lo suficiente y así, antes de haber entrado a su cuarto para verla por última vez con esa sonrisa tan extraña, haber pedido que le colocaran los dientes correctamente y no como lo hicieron antes de poder entrar a su habitación; y luego tendríamos que asegurarnos de que sus cenizas no fueran depositadas por segunda vez en esa especie de vulgar contenedor aéreo dentro del cual fue enviada al norte, al cementerio.

you the wrong advice because his reasons were the same ones he gave you the last time he advised you to get married at eighteen. If you could bring a child from a first marriage into a second marriage a second time, you would know that generosity could turn to resentment if you did not do the right things and resentment back to kindness if you did, unless the man you married when you married a second time for the second time was quite different in temperament from the man you married when you married a second time for the first time, in which case you would have to marry that one twice also in order to learn just what the wisest course would be to take with a man of his temperament. If you could have your mother die a second time you might be prepared to fight for a private room that had no other person in it watching television while she died, but if you were prepared to fight for that, and did, you might have to lose your mother again in order to know enough to ask them to put her teeth in the right way and not the wrong way before you went into her room and saw her for the last time grinning so strangely, and then yet one more time to make sure her ashes were not buried again in that plain sort of airmail container in which she was sent north to the cemetery.

LAS MADRES

჻

LYDIA DAVIS

Translation by Ana Rosa González Matute

Todos tenemos una madre en algún lugar. Durante la cena ella se encuentra entre nosotros. Es una mujer pequeña, con lentes tan gruesos que parecen oscuros cuando voltea. Luego la madre de la anfitriona telefonea mientras cenamos. Por ello la anfitriona se ausenta de la mesa más de lo esperado. Esta madre posiblemente esté en Nueva York. En la conversación se menciona a la madre de uno de los invitados: se halla en Oregon, un estado del que algunos sabemos muy poco, aunque ya ha sucedido que un pariente viva ahí. Más tarde, ya en el auto, se menciona a un coreógrafo. Él pasará la noche en la ciudad; de hecho, estará de paso para ver a su madre que se encuentra en otro lugar.

MOTHERS

ऋ

LYDIA DAVIS

Everyone has a mother somewhere. There is a mother at dinner with us. She is a small woman with eyeglass lenses so thick they seem black when she turns her head away. Then, the mother of the hostess telephones as we are eating. This causes the hostess to be away from the table longer than one would expect. This mother may possibly be in New York. The mother of a guest is mentioned in conversation: this mother is in Oregon, a state few of us know anything about, though it has happened before that a relative lived there. A choreographer is referred to afterwards, in the car. He is spending the night in town, on his way, in fact, to see his mother, again in another state.

. . .

Cuando las madres son las invitadas a una cena comen bien, al igual que los niños, pero parecen ausentes. Suelen no comprender lo que hacemos o decimos. Con frecuencia sucede que participan en la conversación sólo si se habla de cuando éramos jóvenes o intervienen justo cuando no se desea que lo hagan; sonríen y se les malinterpreta. Y sin embargo a las madres siempre se les ve, siempre se les habla, aunque sólo sea en días festivos. Han sufrido por nosotros y con mayor frecuencia en un sitio donde no podíamos verlas.

.   .   .

Mothers, when they are guests at dinner, eat well, like children, but seem absent. It is often the case that they cannot follow what we are doing or saying. It is often the case, also, that they enter the conversation only when it turns on our youth; or they accommodate where accommodation is not wanted; smile and are misunderstood. And yet mothers are always seen, always talked to, even if only on holidays. They have suffered for our sakes, and most often in a place where we could not see them.

LO QUE ELLA SABÍA

∽

LYDIA DAVIS

Translation by Ana Rosa González Matute

La gente ignoraba lo que ella sabía, que en realidad no era una mujer sino un hombre, con frecuencia un hombre gordo y, tal vez aún con más frecuencia, un viejo. El hecho de que ella fuera un viejo le dificultaba ser una mujer joven. Por ejemplo, le era difícil hablar con un hombre joven pese a que se mostrara verdaderamente interesado en ella. Debía preguntarse a sí misma, ¿por qué este joven coquetea con este viejo?

WHAT SHE KNEW

༈

LYDIA DAVIS

People did not know what she knew, that she was not really a woman but a man, often a fat man, but more often, probably, an old man. The fact that she was an old man made it hard for her to be a young woman. It was hard for her to talk to a young man, for instance, though the young man was clearly interested in her. She had to ask herself, Why is this young man flirting with this old man?

DOS HERMANAS

᠅

LYDIA DAVIS

Translation by Ana Rosa González Matute

Si bien nadie desea que ocurra, y sería preferible que no ocurriera, suele suceder que nace una segunda hija y hay dos hermanas.

Por supuesto que cualquier hija, cuando llora a la hora de nacer, es sólo un fracaso, y su padre la recibe con el corazón apesadumbrado porque el hombre deseaba varones. Lo vuelve a intentar: de nuevo sólo una hija. Peor aún ya que se trata de una segunda hija; luego una tercera e incluso una cuarta. Se siente miserable entre hembras. Vive desesperado con sus fracasos.

Afortunado el hombre que tiene un hijo y una hija, aunque el riesgo es mayor al buscar otro varón. Más afortunado el hombre que únicamente tiene varones y puede continuar uno tras otro hasta que nazca la hija; así tendrá todos los hijos que desee y también una pequeña hija para adornar su mesa. Y si ésta

TWO SISTERS

၁

LYDIA DAVIS

Though everyone wishes it would not happen, and though it would be far better if it did not happen, it does sometimes happen that a second daughter is born and there are two sisters.

Of course any daughter, crying in the hour of her birth, is only a failure, and is greeted with a heavy heart by her father, since the man wanted sons. He tries again: again it is only a daughter. This is worse, for it is a second daughter; then it is a third, and even a fourth. He is miserable among females. He lives, in despair, with his failures.

The man is lucky who has one son and one daughter, though his risk is great in trying for another son. Most fortunate is the man with sons only, for he can go on, son after son, until the daughter is made, and he will have all the sons he could wish

nunca llega, entonces ya tiene una mujer en su esposa, la madre de sus hijos. Él en sí mismo no tiene a un hombre. Sólo su esposa lo tiene. Ella, al no tener una mujer, bien podría desear una niña, pero sus deseos casi son inaudibles. Es en sí una hija, aunque sus padres ya no viven.

La hija única, la única hermana entre varios hermanos, escucha la voz de su familia, se siente complacida y feliz. Admiran su ternura frente a la brutalidad de sus hermanos, su calma frente a su destrucción. Pero cuando son dos hermanas, una es más fea y torpe que la otra, una es menos inteligente, una más promiscua. Incluso cuando afloran las mejores cualidades en una de ellas, como suele suceder, ésta no será feliz porque la otra, como una sombra, seguirá su éxito con envidia.

Dos hermanas crecen en distintos momentos y se desprecian entre sí por ser tan infantiles. Discuten y enrojecen. Y si tan sólo hubiera una hija, se llamaría Ángela; en cambio dos perderían sus nombres y en consecuencia se fortalecerían.

Con frecuencia dos hermanas se casan. Una encuentra vulgar al marido de la otra. Ésta utiliza a su esposo como escudo para protegerse de su hermana y del cuñado, a quien teme por su agudeza. Si bien las dos intentan la amistad para que sus hijos tengan primos, continúan distanciadas.

Sus maridos las decepcionan. Los hijos son un fracaso y malgastan el amor de sus madres en parrandas. Sólo el odio de una hacia la otra es duro como el hierro. Esto perdura mientras sus esposos se marchitan y los hijos se alejan.

for and a little daughter as well, to grace his table. And if the daughter should never come, then he has a woman already, in his wife the mother of his sons. In himself he has not a man. Only his wife has that man. She could wish for a daughter, having no woman, but her wishes are hardly audible. For she is herself a daughter, though she may have no living parents.

The single daughter, the many brothers' only sister, listens to the voice of her family and is pleased with herself and happy. Her softness against her brothers' brutality, her calm against their destruction, is admired. But when there are two sisters, one is uglier and more clumsy than the other, one is less clever, one is more promiscuous. Even when all the better qualities unite in one sister, as most often happens, she will not be happy, because the other, like a shadow, will follow her success with green eyes.

Two sisters grow up at different times and despise one another for being such children. They quarrel and turn red. And though if there is only one daughter she will remain Angela, two will lose their names, and be stouter as a result.

Two sisters often marry. One finds the husband of the other crude. The other uses her husband as a shield against her sister and her sister's husband, whom she fears for his quick wit. Though the two sisters attempt friendship so that their children will have cousins, they are often estranged.

Their husbands disappoint them. Their sons are failures and spend their mothers' love in cheap towns. Strong as iron,

Enjauladas, ambas hermanas reprimen su furia. Tienen las mismas facciones.

Dos hermanas vestidas de negro van de compras juntas, los maridos muertos, los hijos muertos en alguna guerra; su odio es tan familiar que ni lo perciben. A veces son tiernas la una con la otra porque olvidan.

Pero al morir, el rostro de las dos hermanas se amarga por costumbre.

only, is now the hatred of the two sisters for one another. This endures, as their husbands wither, as their sons desert.

Caged together, two sisters contain their fury. Their features are the same.

Two sisters, in black, shop for food together, husbands dead, sons dead in some war; their hatred is so familiar that they are unaware of it. They are sometimes tender with one another, because they forget.

But the faces of the two sisters in death are bitter by long habit.

PEOPLE SHOULDN'T HAVE TO BE THE ONES TO TELL YOU

࿓

GARY LUTZ

He had a couple of grown daughters, disappointers, with regretted curiosities and the heavy venture of having once looked alive. One night it was only the older who came by. It was photos she brought: somebody she claimed was more recent. He started approvingly through the sequence. A man with capped-over hair and a face drowned out by sunlight was seen from unintimate range in decorated settings out-of-doors. The coat he wore was always a dark-blue thing of medium hang. But in one shot you could make out the ragged line of a zipper, and in another a column of buttons, and in still another the buttons were no longer the knobby kind but toggles, and in yet another they were not even buttons, just snaps. Sometimes the coat had grown a drawstring. The pockets varied by slant and flapwork. The man advanced through the stack again. His eye this time was caught in doubt by the collar. A contrastive leather in this shot, common corduroy in that one, undiversified cloth in a third. And he was expected to make believe they were all of the same man? He swallowed clumsily, jumbled through the photographs once more.

"But you'll still have time for your sister?" he said.

Her teeth were off-colored and fitted almost mosaicwise into the entire halted smile.

A few nights later, the younger. A night class was making her interview a relation for a memory from way back and then another from only last week. He was not the best person to be in recall, but he thought assistively of a late afternoon he had sat at a table outside a gymnasium and torn tickets off a wheel one at a time instead of in twos and threes for the couples and threesomes. He had watched them file arm in arm into the creped-up place with a revived, stupid sense of how things ought to be done. A banquet? A dance? He never stayed around for things.

He saw his words descend into the whirling ungaieties of her longhand.

"And one from just last week?"

Easier.

At the Laundromat, he had chosen the dryer with a spent fabric-softener sheet teased behind inside it. He brought the sheet home afterward to wonder whether it was more a mysti-cization of a tissue than a denigration of one. It was sparser in its weave yet harder to tear apart, ready in his hand when unthrob-bing things of his life could stand to be swabbed clean.

(He watched his daughter wait a considerate, twingeing minute before she set down the tumbler from which she had been sipping her faucet water.)

"Your sister's the one with the head for memory," he said. "You ever even once think to ask her?"

Most nights, the man's hair released its oils into the antimacassar at the back of his chair. The deepening oval of grease could one day be worth his daughters' touch.

He got the two of them fixed in his mind again.

The older went in for dolled-up solitude but was better at batting around the good in people. Her loves were always ei-ther six feet under or ten feet tall because of somebody else.

The younger was a rich inch more favored in height, but slower of statement. Men, women, were maybe not her type. But she was otherwise an infatuate of whatever you set before her—even the deep-nutted cledges of chocolate she picked apart for bits of skin.

They had tilted into each other early, then eased off, shied aside.

Then they were wifely toward him for a night, poising curtains at his streetward windows, hurrying the wrinkles out from his other good pants, running to the bathroom between turns at his dirt. The older holding the dustpan again, the younger the brush—a stooped, ruining twosome losing balance in his favor.

They were on the sofa afterward, each with a can of surging soda.

"Third wheel," he said, and went into his bedroom to sit. Were there only two ways to think? One was that the day did not come to you whole. It was whiffled. Things were blowing out of it already. Or else a day was actually two half-days, each half-day divided into dozenths, each dozenth corrugated plentifully into its minutes. There was time.

He sat, stumped.

When he looked in on them again, they had already started going by their middle names—hard-pressed, standpat single syllables. Barb and Dot.

The next couple of nights he kept late hours, pulling his ex-wife piecemeal out of some surviving unmindedness. The first night it was only the lay of her shoulders.

On the next: the girlhood browniness still upheld in her hair—a jewelried uprisal of it.

The souse of the cologne she had stuck by.

Budgets of color in her eyelids.

The night it was the downtrail of veins strung in her arms, he had had enough of her to reach at least futilely for the phone.

It was the younger's number he dialed.

It was a different, lower voice he brought the words up

inside of. She had never been one to put the phone down on a pausing stranger.

"People shouldn't have to be the ones to tell you," he said.

One night, he went over their childhoods again. Had he done nearly enough?

Their mother had taught them that you can ask anybody anything, but it can't always be "Do I know you?"

That you had arms to bar yourself from people.

That you had to watch what you touched after you had already gone ahead and touched some other thing first.

That the most pestering thing on a man was the thing that kept playing tricks with how long it actually was.

For his part, he had got it across that a mirror could not be counted on to give its all. If they should ever need to know what they might look like, they were to keep their eyes off each other and come right to him. He would tell them what was there. In telling it, he put flight and force into the hair, nursed purpose into the lips, worked a birthmark into the shape of a slipper.

Each had a room to roam however she saw fit in either fickleness or frailty.

Rotten spots on the flesh of a banana were just "ingrown cinnamon."

The deep well of the vacuum cleaner accepted any runty jewelry they shed during naps.

The house met with cracks, lashings.

They walked themselves to his chair one day as separates, apprentices at the onrolling household loneliness. The older wanted to know whether it was more a help or a hindrance that things could not drop into your lap if you were sitting up straight to the table. The younger just wanted ways to stunt her growth that would not mean spending more money.

When they were older, and unreproduced, he figured they expected him to start taking after them at least a little. So he now and then let his eyes slave away at the backs of his fingers in the manner of the younger. He raised the older's keynote tone of gargly sorrow up as far into his voice as it deserved when it came time again to talk about his car, any occult change in how the thing took a curve.

Some nights he saw his ex-wife's face put to fuming good use on each of theirs. His failings? A waviness around all he felt bad about, a slovenry mid-mouth. Timid, uncivic behaviors that went uncomprehended. Before the layoffs, he'd been a subordinate with at least thorny standing among the otherwise harmable. He had left it to others to take everything the wrong way. (Tidy electrical fires, backups downstairs, wastepaper calculations off by one dim digit.)

From where they had him sitting, to see a thing through meant only to insist on the transparency within it, to regard it as done and gone.

But adultery? It was either the practice, the craft, of going about as an adult, or there had been just that once. Poles above the woman's toilet had shot all the way up to the ceiling, hoisting shelves of pebble-grained plastic. The arc of his piss was at least a suggestion of a path that thoughts could later take. He went back to the bed and found her sitting almost straight up in her sleep. Her leg was drawn forward: a trough had formed between the line of the shin bone and some flab gathered to the side. It needed something running waterily down its course. All he had left in him now was spittle.

At home afterward: unkindred totes and carryalls arranged in wait beside the door. He poked into the closest one to see whose clothing it might be. His fingers came up with the evenglow plush and opponency of something segregatedly hers. A robe, or something in the robe family.

One night he paid a visit to the building where the two of them lived on different floors. First the older: buttons the size of quarters sewn at chafing intervals into the back panels of what she showed him to as a seat. He had to sit much farther forward than ordinarily. He gave her money to take the younger one out for a restaurant supper. "How will I know what she likes?" she said. Then two flights up to the younger, but she was on the phone. A doorway chinning bar hangered with work smocks blocked him from the bedroom. The bathroom door was open. Passages of masking tape stuck to the plastic apparatus of her hygiene, but unlabelled, uncaptioned. Everything smacked of what was better kept to herself. When she got away from the phone, he gave her money to pick something nice out for her sister. "But what?" she said. "You've known her all your life," he said. "But other than that?" she said.

No sooner did he have the two of them turning up in each other's feelings again than his own days gave way underneath.

The library switched to the honor system. You had to sign the books out yourself and come down hard when you botched their return shelving. (He gawked mostly at histories, stout books full of people putting themselves out.) He recovered a gorge of hair from the bathroom drain and set it out on the soap dish to prosper or at least keep up. There were two telephone directories for the hallway table now—the official, phone-company one and the rival, heavier on front matter, bus schedules, seating charts. You had to know where to turn. He began breaking into a day from odd slants, dozing through the lower afternoon, then stepping out onto the platform of hours already packed beneath him. It should have put him on a higher footing. He started collecting sleeveless blouses—"shells" they were called. Was there anything less devouring that a woman could pull politely over herself? The arms swept through the holes and came right out again, unsquandered. He tucked the shells between the mattress pad and the mattress and barged above them in his sleep.

The younger showed up with an all-occasion assortment of greeting cards from the dollar store. She fanned them out on the floor so that only the greetings would show.

"Which ones can't I send?" she said.

"What aren't you to her?" he said.

"I'm not 'Across the Miles.'"

"Mail that when you're at the other end of town, running errands."

Then the movie house in his neighborhood reduced the ticket price to a dollar. It was a thrifty way to do himself out of a couple of hours. He followed the bad-mouthing onscreen or just sat politely until it was time to tip the rail of the side door.

He became a heavier dresser, a coverer.

The older called to say that while the younger was away, she had sneaked inside to screw new brass pulls into the drawerfronts of her bureau.

"It'll all dawn on her," she said.

Before the week wore out, the two of them came by together one night, alike in the sherbety tint to their lips, the violescent quickening to the eyelids. Identical rawhide laces around their necks, an identical paraphernalium (something from a tooth?) suspended from each. Hair toiled up into practically a bale, with elastics. High-rising shoes similar in squelch and hectic stringage. They were both full of an unelevated understanding of something they had each noticed on TV—a substitution in the schedule. He had noticed it too. It hadn't improved him.

They were holding hands.

Each finger an independent tremble.

He had to tell them: "This is not a good time."

How much better to get the door shut against them now!

His nights were divided three ways. This was the hour for the return envelopes that came with the bills. The utilities no longer bothered printing the rubrics "NAME," "STREET," "CITY, STATE, ZIP" before the lines in the upper-left corner. The lines were yours to fill out as you wished.

Tonight: Electric.

_____

_____

_____

He wrote:

Who sees?

Who sees?

Who sees?

The night his car had to be dropped off for repairs, the older one offered to give him a ride home. He faced a windshield-wiper blade braced to its arm by garbage-bag ties. Come a certain age, she was saying, you start thinking differently of the people closest to hand. You dig up what you already know, but you turn it over more gently before bringing it all the way out. It might be no more than that she catches a cold at every change of the seasons. But why had it taken you this long to think the world of it?

He started listening to just the vowelly lining in what she said.

He skipped the casing consonants that made each word news.

It was carolly to him, a croon.

The daughters had wanted their ceremony held in the lunchroom where they worked. Other than him, it was only women who showed—a table's worth of overfragrant, older co-workers. The officiating one, the day supervisor, wanted to first run down her list of what she was in no position to do. It was a long, hounding list of the "including but not limited to" type. (This was not "espousage"; it was not "jointure"; it was "not in anywise matrimoniously unitudinal.") Then she turned to the daughters and read aloud from her folder to steepening effect that no matter where you might stand on whether things should come with time, it was only natural for you to want to close up whatever little space is left between you and whoever has been the most in your way or out of the question all this long while, and let a line finally be drawn right through the two of you on its quick-gone way to someplace else entirely. Nobody was twisting your arm for you to finish what you should have been screaming your lungs out for in public since practically day one.

The kiss was swift but depthening.

Then the reception. He was a marvel for once, waving himself loose from the greetings and salutes every time he realized anew that they were intended for the person beside him, or behind.

CONTRIBUTORS

Geoff Bouvier's recent fictions appear in *New American Writing*, *Barrow Street*, *LIT*, *Conduit*, and *3rd Bed*.

Kim Chinquee received her MA in Creative Writing from the University of Southern Mississippi and is currently completing her MFA at the University of Illinois. Her work has appeared or is forthcoming in *NOON*, *North Dakota Quarterly*, *Denver Quarterly*, and *The Chattahoochee Review*, among others. She received a Henfield Transatlantic Review Award.

Lydia Davis's most recent collection of stories is *Samuel Johnson Is Indignant* (McSweeney's, 2001; an ALA Notable Book). It is available in paperback, out from Picador. Her translation of Marcel Proust's *The Way by Swann's* is scheduled to be published in the UK by Penguin in their Modern Classics series.

Richard Dokey's stories have appeared most recently in *The Literary Review*, *Witness*, and *Harpur Palate*. His novel *The Hollow Man* was published by Delta West.

Bill Hayward is a photographer who lives and works in New York City. His most recent book is *Bad Behavior* (Rizzoli, 2000). *The American Memory Project* is the title of his work in progress. Hayward's website is www.billhayward.com.

Jibade-Khalil-Huffman was born in Detroit, lived in Florida, and is currently finishing his BA in Photography at Bard College.

Gary Lutz is the author of *Stories in the Worst Way* (Knopf)—recently published in paperback by 3rd Bed.

Ana Rosa González Matute was born in Mexico City. She is the author of three books of poetry and the editor of an anthology of contemporary North American short stories, *Un caracol en la Estigia* (Aldus). Her most recent book is her first collection of short stories, *Gneis* (Aldus, 2000).

Ottessa Moshfegh's work has appeared in *Fence*.

Christine Schutt is the author of a collection of stories, *Nightwork*. Her fiction has been published in *Mississippi Review, Alaska Quarterly Review, The Kenyon Review, Denver Quarterly*, and *NOON*, among others. Awards include an O'Henry Prize and Pushcart Prize.

Hendrika Sonnenberg & Chris Hanson were both born in Canada. They have been collaborating for fifteen years and now live and work in New York. They have shown nationally and internationally and are represented in New York by Cohan and Browne.

Deb Olin Unferth's work appears in the *Colorado Review, Willow Springs, StoryQuarterly, The Literary Review*, and elsewhere. She lives in Chicago.

Rick Whitaker is the author of *Assuming the Position: A Memoir of Hustling* (Four Walls Eight Windows). He lives in New York City and is at work on a book about gay writers.

LIST OF ART WORKS

1   THE IMPORTANT THING IS TO GET THINGS OFF THE GROUND
1988
cardboard, wood, debris
56" x 22" x 18"
b&w photograph (edition of 5 + 1AP)

2   AGREEMENT ROOM   1990
b&w photograph (edition 10 + 2AP)

3   WOOD IN TREES   1990
wood, tree
tree size
b&w photograph (edition of 5 + 1AP)

4   FORT   1994
cotton & polyester fabric, foam
user defined dimensions (approx. 50" x 30" x 30")

5   ENTERTAINING PROXIMITY TO MONUMENTS   1999
7" x 5"
c-print (edition of 10 + 1AP)

Chris Hanson and public sculpture, Nordhorn

6   FRUIT BOWL   1998
43¼" x 74¼"
c-print (unique + 1AP)

7   AGREEMENT ROOM   1998
c-print (edition of 10 + 2AP)

8   installing CLOSET ROD at Los Angeles Contemporary Exhibitions

9   LOS STACKOS   1989
    empty Corona, glass
    c-print (edition of 5 + 1AP)

10 AGREEMENT ROOM   2001
    b&w photograph (edition of 10 + 2AP)

11 ROUND TABLE   2002
    cotton & polyester fabric, ribbons, styrene pellets, sand
    approx 10" x 12' diameter

12 DUMPY   2001
    synthetic modeling compound
    3" x 4" x 4"

13 SOAP BOX   2000
    polystyrene, hot glue
    61" x 11" x 11"

14 BAUDELAIRE   1994
    bronze (edition of 3 + 1AP)
    $3\frac{1}{2}$" x $5\frac{1}{2}$" x 4"

The Iowa Review

A NOTE ON THE TYPE

This book was set in Fournier, a typeface named for Pierre Simon Fournier, a celebrated type designer in eighteenth-century France. Fournier's type is considered transitional in that it drew its inspiration from the old style yet was ingeniously innovational, providing for an elegant yet legible appearance. For some time after his death in 1768, Fournier was remembered primarily as the author of a famous manual of typography and as a pioneer of the print system. However, in 1925 his reputation was enhanced when the Monotype Corporation of London revived Fournier's roman and italic.

Bound by Acme Bookbinding
Charlestown, Massachusetts
Typeset and printed by The Stinehour Press
Lunenburg, Vermont
Typography and cover design by Susan Carroll

FENCE

WILL ALEXANDER
ELIZABETH
ALEXANDER
STEVE ALMOND
BRUCE ANDREWS
RAE ARMANTROUT
JOHN ASHBERY
CAL BEDIENT
CHARLES
BERNSTEIN
MICHAEL
BURKARD
LEE ANN BROWN
ANNE CARSON
HELENE CIXOUS
GILLIAN CONOLEY
CLARK COOLIDGE
ROBERT COOVER
MAHMOUD
DARWISH
MARK DOTY
CORNELIUS EADY
RUSSELL EDSON
KENWARD
ELMSLIE
THALIA FIELD
NICK FLYNN
AMY GERSTLER
JORIE GRAHAM

ALLEN
GROSSMAN
BRENDA HILLMAN
FANNY HOWE
CHRISTINE HUME
CLAUDIA KEELAN
WELDON KEES
PAUL LAFARGE
ANN LAUTERBACH
SAM LIPSYTE
JACKSON
MAC LOW
BEN MARCUS
RICK MOODY
JANE MILLER
SUSAN MITCHELL
LAURA MULLEN
HARRYETTE
MULLEN
EILEEN MYLES
GEOFFREY
NUTTER
G.E. PATTERSON
CLAUDIA RANKINE
DONALD REVELL
ADRIENNE RICH
LAURA RIDING
ELIZABETH
ROBINSON
MARY RUEFLE

MURIEL
RUKEYSER
YI SANG
LESLIE SCALAPINO
ELENI SIKELIANOS
JULIANA SPAHR
COLE SWENSEN
WALLACE
STEVENS
JANE UNRUE
JAMES TATE
SAM TRUITT
JEAN VALENTINE
KAREN VOLKMAN
ROSMARIE
WALDROP
MARJORIE WELISH
JOE WENDEROTH
SUSAN WHEELER
DARA WIER
C.D. WRIGHT
MARK
WUNDERLICH
KEVIN YOUNG
DEAN YOUNG

. . . KINDLY
TAKE YOUR
SEAT.

14 Fifth Avenue, #1A New York, NY 10011
www.fencemag.com/www.fencebooks.com

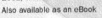

"Gary Lutz is a sentence writer from another planet, deploying language with unmatched invention. He is not just an original literary artist, but maybe the only one to so strenuously reject the training wheels limiting American narrative practice. What results are stories nearly too good to read: crushingly sad, odd, and awe-inspiring." —Ben Marcus

softskull.com

soft skull press

nyc

barking through the night

POST ROAD

MAGAZINE

RECOMMENDATIONS ★ ETCETERA

THEATRE ★ NONFICTION

CRITICISM ★ POETRY

ART ★ FICTION

Subscriptions, $16.00
send check c/o:

POST ROAD
853 BROADWAY
SUITE 1516, BOX 85
NYC, NY 10003

http://webdelsol.com/Post_Road

"A very young poet who seems to have acquired
a lifetime of experience while retaining a vast
empathy (without a trace of sappiness) is a rare thing.
These carefully calibrated poems have narratives,
and form an autobiography; they have the suspense
and fullness of short stories with knockout final lines.
The locale may be specific (Midwest, semi-rural), the
voice (adolescence on the cusp of adulthood) and
themes (family, desire, exile) recognizable, but
T. Cole Rachel makes the mundane feel urgent,
fresh, vital. This is powerful writing by a witness
wise beyond his years. The gripping poems are so
good that you find yourself wanting the writer to
try his hand at everything: films, novels, songs,
plays—they all seem within his reach."

Bret Easton Ellis

SURVIVING THE MOMENT OF IMPACT
T. Cole Rachel

"It is a fierce hymn of a nearly cannibalistic
passion for the people he has loved against all odds."

Edmund White

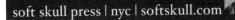

soft skull press | nyc | softskull.com

THE PARIS REVIEW

Ernest Hemingway   E.M. Forster   Vladimir Nabokov
Norman Mailer   Allen Ginsberg   Italo Calvino   T.S. Eliot
Rick Bass   Dorothy Parker   John Updike   James Merrill
William Faulkner   Elizabeth Bishop   Tennessee Williams
Robert Bly   Lillian Hellman   T.C. Boyle   Sam Shepard
Anne Sexton   James Baldwin   Arthur Miller   Don DeLillo
Harold Bloom   Robert Frost   Neil Simon   P.L. Travers
Thornton Wilder   Jeffrey Eugenides   William Styron
Shelby Foote   Jean Cocteau   William Carlos Williams
Geoffrey Hill   Simone   Martin McDonagh
John Dos Passos   William S. Burroughs
Philip Roth   Robert Penn Warren   Mark Strand   Woody Allen
John le Carré   Frank O'Hara   Gabriel García Márquez
Wendy Wasserstein   E.L. Doctorow   Margaret Atwood
Eugène Ionesco   Ezra Pound   Toni Morrison   Iris Murdoch
Raymond Carver   John Hollander   Alain Robbe-Grillet
Philip Larkin   August Wilson   V.S. Naipaul   José Saramago
John Ashbery   Terry Southern   Günter Grass   Martin Amis
Milan Kundera   Joan Didion   Jack Kerouac   Octavio Paz
Donald Hall   Tom Wolfe   Peter Matthiessen   John Guare
Marianne Moore   Ken Kesey   John Irving   Kurt Vonnegut
Pablo Neruda   John Cheever   Tom Stoppard   Jim Carroll
David Mamet   W.H. Auden   Harold Pinter   A.R. Ammons
Judy Budnitz   Denis Johnson   Anne Carson   Rick Moody

SINCE 1953

www.parisreview.com • 718.539.7085 • distributed by Eastern News

CONJUNCTIONS:39

THE NEW WAVE FABULISTS

A landmark anthology devoted to science fiction, horror, and fantasy

Guest-edited by Peter Straub

New work by John Crowley, Jonathan Carroll, Karen Joy Fowler, Joe Haldeman, Neil Gaiman, Elizabeth Hand, Jonathan Lethem, Andrew Duncan, John Clute, Nalo Hopkinson, M. John Harrison, Kelly Link, John Kessel, China Miéville, James Morrow, Patrick O'Leary, Geoff Ryman, Gary K. Wolfe, Peter Straub, and others. 360 pages, $15.

CONJUNCTIONS

Edited by Bradford Morrow
Published by Bard College
Annandale-on-Hudson, NY 12504
(845) 758-1539

Visit www.conjunctions.com

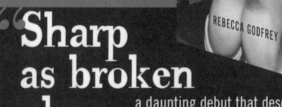